AF506395

Her & Him

Matthew Lester

Copyright © 2024 Matthew Lester

All rights reserved.

No part of this publication may be reproduced, distributed, or transmitted in any form or by any means, including photocopying, recording, or other electronic or mechanical methods, without the prior written permission of the publisher, except as permitted by U.S. copyright law.

The story, all names, characters, and incidents portrayed in this production are fictitious. No identification with actual persons (living or deceased), places, buildings, and products is intended or should be inferred.

Contents

Chapter 1

She suddenly threw the covers back and, in an instant, sat up on the edge of the bed. Feelings of sadness, frustration, and anger rushed through her mind, all at once. Dreams like that were disorienting. It took her a moment to realize where she was, when it was, and that the dream that awakened her could never be reality. As her thoughts cleared and her emotions calmed, she gazed past the sliding glass doors that led to the balcony, and let her ears fill with the sound of the Atlantic gently lapping against the sand.

The tide was going out.

She had lived in harmony with the sea, becoming so familiar with it that she could tell the tides by the sounds of the waves. The reality of her daily existence began to settle in, and she noticed the faint gold of daybreak upon the horizon. Usually, this was a time she gladly escaped each day. Most nights, she could not fall asleep until the witching hours had begun and usually remained in a dream-like state until the morning grew late. The early hours of the day had been a struggle for quite some time. As a child and going into adulthood, she would usually rise before the sun, looking optimistically for whatever the day might bring. That optimism and her love of the morning had all died ten years ago, tomorrow.

The dream that had brought her out of bed was not a nightmare but a reality lived often in times long past. She would wake with her head comfortably resting on her grandmother's old feather pillow, her left leg extended, and her right leg slightly bent with her foot outside the covers. Her arms would be curled with her hands next to her face. He always snuggled up to her with his right leg over hers and his arm wrapped around her body while holding her arm near her wrist with his hand. His warm breath on her neck usually awakened her, and she would lay there motionless until his alarm went off and he would get out of bed.

This morning, her mind and body had betrayed her. The peaceful sleep she was experiencing was not a normal thing for her. Sleep, when it came, was usually filled with twitches, aches, and a temperature that made her wonder if something more serious might be wrong. Night sweats, nightmares, and restlessness were her normal.

Not today.

This morning he was there, as real as he had been ten years ago. What must have lasted only seconds felt like an eternity until the cruel timer of reality sounded to awaken her and face the truth of what each day now brought.

Loneliness.

She walked onto the balcony, watching the sun, a bright red ball of fire, rising past its retreat. The beach below was empty. Only the clamor of seabirds in their pursuit of food stirred the calmness. She looked towards Hilton Head to see if any cargo ships were passing and, witnessing an unchanging expanse of blue, turned to look towards the pier. This small expanse of the balcony from where she viewed the world was her favorite place on earth, and she had it all to herself.

As the sun cleared the horizon, something caught her eye. She was not exactly sure how she had missed him. She watched as he turned violently as if throwing something at the sun, yet nothing left his hand. Then, he turned to walk towards the pier. Perhaps it was because of his white linen trousers and a white shirt that blended in with the sand, or because of his nigh motionless stance–or for reasons entirely unknown to her, she immediately resented him for sharing this morning without her permission. Some guy dressed like the cover of a romance novel standing between her and the sun, disrupting her peace. She watched him walk until he disappeared under the pier, wishing in her heart that it were the edge of the Earth.

She went inside to make a cup of coffee. Grabbing her phone, she returned to the balcony to see what interesting things would be on social media and relax before her shift began. She was a waitress, not out of necessity or because it was her chosen vocation. No, she was a waitress because she could work at her favorite restaurant, a little seafood place with most of the seating on a deck out back, overlooking the Back River. The job gave her something to do to occupy her time, required little to no mental effort, and allowed her to watch the sunset on the marsh each day, and for a while, be distracted from the emptiness of the house. Her shift didn't start till eleven, so she had hours to kill before she rode her bicycle to work.

The trip took fifteen minutes, and she parked her bike next to the giant chairs in front of the restaurant, not worried if it would be there when her shift ended.

She walked into work as she normally did, wearing shorts, a t-shirt, and her hair in a ponytail. Pam had owned the restaurant for decades. She had been there nine years and Pam was there long before that. Pam was in her sixties with features that revealed a strong woman with a sun-weathered face and a determination few men possessed. She had survived hurricanes, floods, and the good or bad fortune of being married to the same man for over forty years. It was her stability–an anchor to a place and occupation that she truly admired and needed from her. Pam had given her a job when they met on the pier during the offseason. She had been walking aimlessly before stopping at the end of the pier and leaning on the rail, facing the ocean so no one could see her tears.

Pam had walked up to her and asked what was wrong, thinking she had been assaulted or perhaps was three sheets to the wind. She turned to Pam and, with a trembling voice, explained that it was her anniversary. Pam was not an emotional person, but everything in her being caused her to reach out and embrace this young woman. The pain she saw was the type that did not need to be explained and could not be comforted. Pam just held her and said, "Walk with me."

She did not know this woman, but her voice sounded strong and sincere. She walked with her and was unaware of the direction or distance they were going until they were at the entrance to a restaurant. It was closed, but Pam had a key to the door. She seated her at the bar, and asked, "What's your poison?"

When there was no answer, Pam quickly mixed a pitcher of Margaritas and poured them a drink. Through the first glass, no one spoke. Finally, she said, "This is my first anniversary without my husband." Pam shook her head but did not reply–the sympathy she felt showed on her face. Whether it was the tequila or just a sympathetic ear, she told her story to Pam.

Nathaniel had been a senior when she was a freshman and had been the only upperclassman to even pretend to know she existed. They shared a math class since he had failed it and chose to sit behind her. He thought she was cute but more importantly, she looked smart, which could come in handy.

Nate was on the high school football team and had never been a starter but was enthusiastic about the game. He occasionally subbed in when the score got out of hand.

Everyone in high school knew him because while he lingered on the bench in the fall, in the spring, he would be the defending state champion on the wrestling team. As a wrestler, his five-six height and one hundred and twenty-five-pound weight were not setbacks; he was a beast. She had always thought she wanted to date a much taller boy. Since she stood five feet and four inches tall and usually wore heels, the pictures would look funny if she was taller than her date. That thought did not enter her head during math class that fall when he tapped her shoulder and asked if she wanted to be his date for homecoming. She had never been on a date before and quickly said, "Yes." Only later in the day did she remember that her father had said 'no' to dating until she was sixteen. She still had ten months left. She had waited for him to come out of the locker room after practice to tell him that he had to stop by her house to ask her father's permission. Nate said he would, and she ran to the parking lot where her mother was waiting to take her home. She had never ridden the bus; her mother quit her nursing job after she was born to stay home with her. When she started school, her mother got a job in a doctor's office so she could always be available to take her only child to school.

It was six thirty when her doorbell rang, and her father got up to see the boy who had asked his daughter to the dance. His mind was made up already. The answer would be 'No.' When he opened the door, Nate surprised him by extending his hand, and for a small guy, had quite a strong grip. Nate then asked if he could come in. This boy looked ridiculous. His hair was longer than most boys, his wife-beater t-shirt was still wet with sweat, and the shorts he was wearing with the school logo were only touching him at the waist and had they not been tied, would probably have fallen off. But the coup de grace was the Georgia boots on his feet.

This was not a good first impression. The TV was tuned to a sports show where the matches for the weekend MMA fights were being discussed. Nate turned to her dad and asked, "Do you like MMA?" Harold replied that he did and explained that he had always been a fan. Soon they were discussing fights and events, and Nate told him about his wrestling experience. She had told her father Nate was a benchwarmer on the football team but nothing about him being a wrestler. How could she since he had not told her yet? There was a confidence about Nate that most young men did not possess till much later in life, if ever. Harold surprised even himself when he told Nate he could take his daughter to the dance, provided she was home before eleven. This boy was easy to like. Nate said, "Thank you. I will have her home before eleven," and stood up to leave. He walked into the kitchen to say hi to her mom and that he looked forward to seeing her in math class tomorrow.

She realized she was in her room but did not remember going up the stairs; perhaps she had floated. This was going to be her first date, and she couldn't wait to tell Karen.

These memories quickly flooded her for a moment, allowing the grief to subside and her lips to form a smile. She looked at Pam and explained that Nate was her first date, her first dance, her first kiss, her first everything. When she could speak again, she told Pam how they dated while he was in college and that they both graduated the same summer. After graduation night, he took her to their favorite restaurant. Once they finished dinner, he got down on his knee, right in the middle of the crowd, and asked her to marry him. She did not notice the ring or the loud applause from everyone seated near them. There was only the look in his eyes and her own tears as she said, mostly shrieking, "Yes." In the car, on the way home, she took a closer look at the ring. *Wow, this is big,* she thought, and it was. Two and a half carats mounted in a beautiful white gold setting. While she thought she knew everything about Nate, what she didn't know was that he had been saving for this ring since that first date in ninth grade. She also didn't know he had spent ten thousand dollars on this ring and kept it a secret since Christmas. He would tell her later, but that would only lead to her loving him more.

The wedding would be in the fall of the next year. Nate was in Army ROTC and his training would begin in September. He had been commissioned the same day he graduated and, my God, he looked great in those dress blues. They were married on Columbus Day. Her wedding day was a blur and she only had one memory of the ceremony; they had prepared their vows and while hers were nice, his brought several women who were not crying to tears. He started by telling her he had known that he would marry her since the homecoming dance during her freshman year. The kiss they shared at the end of the last slow dance of the night was the best kiss he had ever experienced, and she would be the last woman he would ever kiss. He had started planning and saving for this day on his way home from that first date.

If only he had gone home, he had thought to himself.

After the guests had gone and the evening was settling down, he told her there was a surprise. No matter how much she begged, he would not say. He just told her to get in his old truck. They said goodbye to their parents and then drove away from the officers' club where the wedding and reception had been. Soon, they were off post and headed towards Savannah. When they turned onto

Presidential Parkway, she knew they were headed towards Tybee and begged him to tell her, but he just smiled. When they crossed the bridge onto the island, he said, "Not much further now." Just before the curve where Highway Eighty turned into Butler Avenue, they turned left. This was a gated condominium complex.

Why are we here, she thought.

Nate reached into his pocket and took out a key card. They went around the pools to a building at the north end of the complex. Together, they walked up the stairs at the end of the building and climbed to the third floor. After opening the door, he carried her over the threshold and said, "Welcome home." Nate's father was a real estate broker and when the market had turned down a couple of years before, they had bought this place. It was Nate's wedding gift, along with the mortgage. The place was nice. A two-bed two-bath condo with a fantastic unobstructed view of the ocean and no neighbors above them. *It did need some work,* she thought, but not for long. Nate did not stop to give her a tour of the place or even a look from the balcony. He was taking her to bed.

"And?" Pam asked. "What happened after he said he had a surprise?"

Her mind had continued, but she had stopped talking. Pam's question had interrupted her dress falling to the floor.

"Nate and his dad had bought a condo on the north end of the island. It is where I still live," she said.

The flat, emotionless tone of her sentence told Pam more than she had said. It was not just a beach house, nor just a condo. It was a prison.

The story continued that Nate had gotten word his unit was redeploying to Afghanistan and he would have to leave on their anniversary. This would be his third deployment and she noticed a change in his expression. He had been to Iraq with the Third Infantry Division as a platoon leader and the deployment had been relatively uneventful except for the time apart. He had been able to Skype call her, and that deployment had been the most difficult since it was their first time being separated by combat. For his second deployment, he was a company commander with the Eighty-Second Airborne Division. Although there was more combat action, he never spoke about it. She could tell that deployment had changed him. His moods were darker, he smiled less, and he tended to be very aware of his surroundings. Later. she would learn that those were all signs of PTSD.

This deployment should have been easier since he was the battalion S-2 officer. He said supply officer, but usually, he called them 'bean counters.' "Nothing worse for a combat soldier," he said, "than riding a desk." Also, he was back with the Third Infantry Division, so this was a return to Hinesville and their beach house she loved and missed while they were at Ft. Bragg. They also got post housing this time–rank does have some privileges.

She had woken up that morning in her usual position. On her left side with him right beside her. This morning would be quick and difficult for them both. No time for any hanky-panky–that had been well taken care of the night before. This morning was business and every time he deployed, it was becoming more difficult for her to say goodbye, so he hugged her longer than usual before kissing her, telling her he loved her, and driving away. She always walked him to his truck, that same old truck he had in high school. He could never bring himself to sell or trade it. For him, whenever he looked at the passenger's seat, she was always there. As his truck disappeared, she turned to go back inside her apartment. Suddenly, there was a feeling of such sadness and anguish that she ran to her phone to make sure he was okay. He was barely at the first traffic light when his phone rang. He thought about driving back, but he reassured her, She seemed to be over whatever it was after being comforted, so he made his turn, heading to his battalion.

This deployment was progressing as anticipated, and the end was getting closer.

He had left on their anniversary and sometimes deployments would end a week or two early. She was hoping it would anyway because it was the day after Labor Day and the offseason at Tybee was their favorite time of year. The weekend had been spent cleaning up the condo because that is where they would spend the first seventy-two hours when he got back.

He never called her when he returned from deployments. He just drove home and said, "I'm back." So, when she heard a car door close in the driveway, she was excited and started hurrying towards the garage door. Then, she heard a second car door shut. When she opened the door, no one was there and at that instant, the front doorbell rang. No one ever used that door. As she made her way around the corner of the entryway to the living room, she remembered Nate telling her that if anything ever happened to him, the chaplain and another officer would inform her. As she opened the front door, the first thing she saw was a shiny cross on the lapel of a jacket. Her entire world just collapsed, and she could not speak or move.

The Major asked if they could come inside. She nodded while escorting them to the living room. She did not know Major Kowalski but recognized him as a chaplain. Captain Johns was a person she did know. He had been a lieutenant with her husband at infantry school and was a platoon leader in the Third Infantry Division with Nate during their first deployment years earlier.

The Major was somber but composed. Captain Johns tried to explain, but as a tear ran down his face, his voice trailed off. The only words that came out of his mouth were, "I'm so sorry."

Pam was not talking; if she were an emotional woman, tears would have been streaming from her eyes while the pitcher of margaritas was now down to the last two glasses. As they finished the drinks, she explained that his Humvee had been passing an old wreck on the road outside of Camp Leatherneck when an IED exploded. A coffin had been delivered for the funeral and burial, but it was empty. The worst part was that she never got to see him again. There was no him to see. The explosion had blown the Humvee into pieces. The driver and Nate had to be separated by DNA, for what little of them both that remained.

Pam said, "You have to come back tomorrow and start working here. It'll do you some good." Then she motioned her to follow. They went outside and much to the young woman's amazement, Pam showed her the huge house she lived in, right next door. Pam said, "Come with me, I'll take you home."

The golf cart looked a lot like a big-wheeled off-road truck, but it was a golf cart. Everyone on the island knew who it belonged to and that it might be a good idea to leave it alone. Pam knew how to structure her profanity for the desired effect, and she always carried a three-eighty in a fanny pack she was never without.

The drive was short, but the stairs were difficult, especially since there were two staircases and they kept moving. Pam helped her to the door and ensured she was inside before telling her to come work with her. The young woman said something that was not intelligible and then lay on the sofa. Pam closed the door and drove home, hoping this new friend would return.

The next day she came to the restaurant on her bicycle and every Friday, Saturday, and Sunday since. She only worked weekends since the Savannah VA was where she worked as a receptionist during the week. There were sick days and vacation days available whenever she wanted to take them, but she had not taken a day off for nine years except for Federal holidays, and only if they did not fall on a weekend. Weekends were not work; they were therapy. Today was a beautiful Sunday. This would be a great shift, even though tomorrow would be the worst day of the year. Tomorrow was Columbus Day, and this year, it was on the ninth, the same as her wedding, the same day he left, the last time she ever kissed him.

Her shift was slow and uneventful, but that was about to change.

Chapter 2

Some wounds require specific bandages, and this is especially true when it comes to the heart. The loss of a loved one and the accompanying grief can typically only be bandaged by time. Regret is an open wound that often has no bandage. It is a wound re-inflicted every day and only distraction can prevent its occurrence, however that remedy is temporary. The only cure is forgiveness, but forgiving yourself…

"Damn it," he yelled at the top of his lungs, but no one heard him. The house was empty now and even emptier without her. It was twenty minutes till sunrise, and it took him thirteen minutes to walk to the spot. Worse still, he was going to have to walk in wet clothes. He had washed them and put them in the dryer but only thought he turned it on. They were still wet, but come hell or high water, he was wearing them. This was the most ridiculous outfit she had ever bought him. White linen three-quarter pants and a pirate-looking white shirt. She said it made him look awesome. He tried it on but swore he would never wear it and that weekend, he did not. He threw it on a shelf in his closet and decided that it would rot there. The week of the Fourth of July holiday was over today, and he was not wearing that. Instead, he grabbed his shorts, a shirt, and they went for a walk.

That day was as haunting as an apparition from the most terrifying horror movies. Why was he such an ass? Why didn't he consider her opinions? Why did he get angry at things that didn't even matter? Why didn't he wear that damn outfit for her? Why? The day would be hot, sunny, with a nice breeze, and as perfect as a day could be. They walked hand in hand as they always did, stopping at the north end of the island.

"This is it," she said. "The most beautiful spot on the face of the earth."

The sun was breaking over the horizon and while he thought there were better locations, it did not cross his mind that she would never stand there with him again. They stood there until the sun rose above the water. He kissed her in the gentle glow of the sun and said, "Let's go get breakfast".

He marked the spot and now he was standing there again in these ridiculous clothes, but at least they were mostly dry now. The further he walked, the less ridiculous he felt, and that feeling was being replaced by another emotion, anger. A smoldering fury only tempered from raging into an uncontrollable inferno by the grief and regret that accompanied it. It was good that no one was on the beach that morning. It would not have taken much to set him off and he was capable of extreme violence. As the sun rose degree by degree this morning, his anger at himself for not wearing these clothes for her kept raging. He denied her something so simple, a slight request, and it was so easy to do. He was doing it now.

Only it was too late.

She was gone.

Just as the sun cleared the sea, the clasp on his watch came undone for the ninety-seventh time. It was a watch he had bought for himself years before. *This watch would come loose no more,* he thought to himself. He snatched it from his wrist and threw it at the sun for all he was worthwhile, screaming a word that did not exist in any language. Then, he turned and started walking towards his house. He walked until he passed the pier, and slightly over a quarter of a mile remained to his house. He needed a release from his emotions, so he started to run and by the time he reached his house, it was a full sprint, but not enough effort had been expended.

The shower on the deck had gotten a lot of use since they had remodeled the house because she always made him take off his clothes to shower before he entered the house to keep the sand out. He quickly took off the pants and the shirt. The water felt good, but he was still fuming. There was a workout room with weights, an elliptical, and a treadmill, but today it would be the heavy bag. With his gloves tightly strapped to his hands, he started to punch the bag. He hit it as hard as he could for as long as he could, and this morning, the ordeal lasted eight minutes. He was exhausted and sat on his weight bench until he could catch his breath before stepping into the shower.

He was not one to let his emotions take control of him, which is true if you didn't count anger. He could explode in an instant and break things or bones, but tears were something he didn't do. His father had him late in life and compared to him, his life had been all peaches and cream. As a boy, whenever he had a slight injury, his father's response was always the same "If blood ain't squirting or a bone ain't sticking out, just rub some dirt on it and stop whining like a girl." This statement was usually followed up by "I've had worse than that on my eye." The last statement was true. His father had lost the use of his right eye as a child due to an accident with a steel spring and had cataract surgery on his left eye as an adult to restore his vision. This was not laser surgery like they do now. It was experimental in the fifties, done with a scalpel, and only done at Emory University Hospital in Atlanta. His recovery took weeks and even after the surgery, he had to wear bifocals. Even with his improved eyesight, his father suffered from a sensitivity to light, a suffering that only ended with his death.

His thoughts of the morning and his father's voice were not very consoling as he stood in the cool water of the shower, but his anger gave way to grief, and he just stood there crying. The tears seemed to wash over his anger and for whatever reason, he tried to remember the last time he cried.

He turned the water off and completed his morning rituals. Cargo shorts and a T-shirt. He went to the living room, watched the waves for a moment, then turned on the TV from his recliner. The programming didn't matter. Then it came to him.

Dixie.

Not the name of the South or anything with racial or political overtones, but a stupid dog. His daughter had been given a puppy by a girl in her sophomore class and instead of the girl's mother handing the dog to Elaine, she had handed it to his wife, Virginia. That was a mistake. Technically the dog belonged to his daughter, but that would never be the case. In reality, it belonged to Virginia. Elaine had friends, softball, soccer, and tons of stuff to do outside the house, Virginia had always been a stay-at-home mom and Dixie would be her new baby. Ugly did not begin to describe 'Dixie.' He had heard women bantering about other women's children before and the statement that came to his mind was 'so ugly they were cute'. What a ridiculous statement.

The little dog was tiny and fit in his wife's hand. Solid black except for a white diamond in the center of her chest. Ears that stood up and flattened out like a nun's habit, much like the one an actress wore in the seventies show 'The Flying Nun.' In addition to the ears, the dog was part Boston Terrier and part something, and whatever that other something was, she had a smashed-in face and bugged-out eyes. Eyes that were usually expressing a need for sympathy or complete and utter contempt.

Dixie had been her dog and by the time they had moved to Savannah for his last teaching job, she was seven years old. Their kids were grown, married with lives of their own, so now they could plan to retire after two more years. This would be the first teaching job where he would not be coaching. His life had been consumed for the past twenty-three years with football, baseball, golf, and now they would have time together to enjoy each other's company and see if they still liked each other. That had been his plan. However, when a new football coach was hired at Islands High

School, and he needed a linebacker coach and a baseball coach, instead of speaking to him about the positions, he went straight to the boss, Virginia. She knew her husband enjoyed coaching and had willingly allowed him to pursue his passion for coaching until now. Virginia laughed when she told Coach Mullen she did not mind if her husband joined his staff. Besides, he and Coach Mullen had coached together before, and their sons had played ball together.

Initially, they had moved to an apartment on Wilmington Island while they renovated their house in Tybee. It was on the South end of the island where the Back River flowed into the Atlantic. From the deck on the roof, you could watch the sunrise and sunset, which they often did. They had never lived there but had it in good rental condition and the renters over the past twenty-plus years had paid it off for them while providing a tidy sum of money for renovations. He worked during the week and they would go shopping; to River Street, to different restaurants. The weekends were spent working at the house. It had been a year and a half, so the renovations were almost done. They would be moving into the house as soon as the kitchen was finished, which would take till February. The cabinet maker took an incredible amount of time to install the cabinets. Then the butcher block counters could be installed, and the kitchen completed. The appliances were in the living room like impatient shoppers, waiting their turn in line. He had lined them up in order of installation. Everything was moving according to their plan until the day after the Martin Luther King holiday.

He had not gotten out of bed yet and was enjoying the calm of the morning before he would have to get dressed and then drive to Islands High. Her face was contorted with pain as she entered the bedroom.

"Come here," she begged him. There was such an urgency to her voice that he didn't even put on his pajamas. He rushed straight to the living room, naked.

"Is she breathing?" Virginia had asked, fully knowing the answer, she just needed him to say it.

He stood up after placing his hand on Dixie's chest, but she had died much earlier, perhaps right after they went to bed. She was still on her side as she always slept, but rigor mortis had already begun. He put his arms around her and said, "No girlfriend, she ain't." The tears were freely flowing from her eyes which was difficult enough, but the sadness in her voice telling him all the things that 'Dixie' was to her was too much. Three women in this world had the keys to the lock he kept around his heart, his wife, his daughter, and his mother. A woman's tears were his kryptonite and a weapon for which he had no defense.

He did not know why, but for a reason he could not explain, he thought about their mortality. She was crying and inconsolable while looking at her Dixie lying on her doggie bed as if she were sleeping. He rose to his feet from beside her and pulled her to him, embracing her like he had not done in quite some time. The thought that had occurred to him caused feelings of fear and dread. *What if it was him and not just a dog? He knew she loved him deeply and always said he was her prince charming, but what if he suddenly died?*

He pulled her away from their embrace, wiped the tears from her eyes, and told her, "You must die before me. The thought of your grief and inconsolable sorrow combined with the eternal separation is more than I can imagine. I cannot accept a world where you are alone without me, and no one is there to comfort you. The thought of you weeping without me holding you is causing me much more pain than the loss of that dog."

She stopped crying. She stopped moving. For a moment, she stopped breathing. Her reaction was to kiss him more passionately than she had in quite some time. While he was not a sentimental or openly emotional man, this was the most beautiful expression of love she had ever heard or read.

He fell asleep thinking about her kissing him that day. And for a while, there was no grief, only peaceful sleep, something he had not had in quite some time. When he did wake, some idiot was shouting on the TV about a damn boat made from screen wire and a miracle product that he could get two of for the low, low price of nineteen ninety-five. He could not turn it off fast enough and realized it was afternoon.

His phone showed six missed calls from his children, but more importantly, it was a quarter to five and he had not eaten all day. He grabbed his wallet and texted his kids that he was okay and was just about to eat supper. Then, he walked out of the house towards their favorite restaurant. It would be the first time he had been there without her; they had always stopped there for lunch.

After a short ten-minute walk, he was there. Because it was not crowded, he sat in his preferred seat at the end of the deck. Nothing should be between him and the sunset over the marsh except a cold beer.

Chapter 3

Pam came from the kitchen with an order and told her that a customer was sitting on the deck. He looked pretty much like anyone else who came in, with notable exceptions. Usually, men his age, fiftyish, came in with families or friends. They were also usually out of shape and looked as if, her mother used to say, "his get up and go has got up and went."

When she approached the table, he was watching a pelican make his dive. He loved watching them fish and could watch them for hours.

"Can I get you something to drink?" she asked. She also noticed that his shirt did not protrude from the middle-age spread or beer belly. Instead, it was his chest and shoulders that stood out.

Without looking at her, he replied, "Yes. A pelican." *A what?* he paused at his own answer. He was an idiot. He turned away from the bird and said, "I'm sorry, how about a Miller Lite, a glass of tea, and another beer when you bring out the food." He also noticed a beautiful woman with a distant look, smiling but still disengaged.

She had smiled when he said the first two words, and was still smiling when he turned to give her his attention. She asked him if he knew what he wanted to order. While she had never seen him before, many customers were familiar with the menu and knew their order. His accent let her know he was a local, or at least from Georgia. His face was solid and his eyes a piercing blue-gray. His military-style haircut told her a lot about him. Straight to the point, no fluff, all business.

"Yes," he said. "A cup of she-crab stew, a shrimp and scallop plate, with fries and coleslaw."

She could tell that he had been there before and as he finished ordering, he turned to see another pelican make his dive.

"I'll get those drinks right out to you," she said.

When she got back to the bar, she asked Pam if she had ever seen him come in. While Pam was a people person, she was not a person-person. People came and went, regular customers who had dined there for years might get some recognition, but all the men were 'handsome,' and all the women were 'honey.'

"Not that I remember." Pam said.

Chuck, the bartender, said, "He's been in here but usually at lunch, and with a strikingly-pretty, platinum-haired woman." It was Chuck's business to know people. If you came in twice in the same month, he knew your name and beverage. Chuck was another soul who found refuge at the restaurant. He lived in one of the smallest houses on the island, inherited from his grandfather. Chuck looked to be in his sixties and shortly after he served in Vietnam, he came to the island to re-cooperate. His recovery had taken fifty-plus years so far. He did not get paid a salary, only tips. Since that was the case, he became one of the most attentive bartenders anywhere.

When she took his food to him, he thanked her and bowed his head to pray.

That was a bit unusual, she thought, *drinking a beer, and praying*; unusual, at least, for her. Then, he opened the beer and took a long drink.

She had stopped talking while he was praying and asked if he needed anything else.

"No," he said, turning to his meal.

"I'll check back with you later," she said before heading back in.

She didn't check back on him though. The restaurant got busy. When a couple came in with nowhere to seat them, she noticed he was still sitting there.

"Can I get you anything else?" She asked.

"Another beer."

She noticed that he had only eaten half the stew. All three packs of crackers were opened, but three were still on the plate. The shrimp was all there with half the fries, the coleslaw was only half eaten, and the tea glass was still full.

"Was everything all right?" she asked.

He said, "Yes, it was excellent, as always."

"But you didn't touch the shrimp," she commented.

When he turned to look at her, it was as if he were about to kill her. His face was cold and emotionless. There was no trace of human kindness or compassion. She was starting to move backward from his stare when he spoke.

His voice cracked as the fierceness in his expression turned to something she immediately recognized. Pain.

"They're not mine," he said.

Oh. OH! She understood the woman Chuck had mentioned was his wife, and she had passed away. They were like those couples she had always complained about who shared meals. Which also usually meant meager tips. She had just never seen a couple made up of one.

This is not how work was supposed to be, she thought. Not once in nine years had this ever happened. Her pain and emotions were locked up and buried in those margaritas Pam had made years ago. She could not look at him anymore and, without speaking, turned to run out of the restaurant, yelling to Pam that she had to go home.

Pam was furious. *What the hell had that bastard done to provoke such a reaction from her friend?*

When Pam got to his table, she tried to keep from shouting, but her voice was stern when she asked him what happened.

He did not like her tone and quickly said, "Nothing."

There was no pain in his expression now. He followed with, "She asked me why I didn't eat the shrimp"?

"Well, what was wrong with them?" Pam asked, still in the tone he found annoying.

I simply told her, "They weren't mine."

Pam, now puzzled, asked with her tone a bit softer, "Whose were they?"

Now he was really annoyed. "Look lady, I don't know what kind of weirdos you have working here, but I'm telling you everything that happened. And as for whose shrimp those are, what the hell is it to you? Just give me my damn check."

His tone was commanding, and although she still did not understand, she believed he was telling the truth. She told him he could pay at the bar.

No sunset was worth all this grief, so he got up and went to pay.

"What the hell is wrong with the women in this place," he asked Chuck.

"I don't know man, I've never seen her react like that before, what did you say to her?"

"Like I told the crazy old bat."

"That crazy old bat is the owner," Chuck interrupted.

"I don't care if she is the owner or not, when the nut job waitress asked me why I didn't eat the shrimp, all I said was they weren't mine."

Chuck understood completely. He paused for a moment, looking carefully at the man at the bar. "Hey man," he said. "Didn't you used to come in here a while back with an attractive platinum-haired woman?"

"I don't want to go into all that. Just tell me the damage," he said with a look of surprise.

Chuck said it was thirty-eight seventy-five.

He opened his wallet and handed Chuck one hundred and forty dollars. "When the crazy waitress comes back, please give her the change," he said, then walked out.

Today was turning into complete shit, he thought. All he had wanted was something familiar, a good meal, a quiet evening, and a relaxing sunset. *That ain't too much to ask,* he thought. He also thought that the bartender was sharp as hell. It had been over a year since he was there last, and the bartender had remembered them. All the times they had been in there, he had hardly ever noticed there was a bartender. They always sat on the deck and never had much interest in anyone else around them. Together, they shared their meal in peace and left quietly. At least that was the last meal they had shared there before…

He changed his train of thought. *Nope, not going there anymore today.* There was wine, brandy, tequila, bourbon, and rum waiting on him at his house. The closer he got, the more it looked like a brandy night. He just wanted to relax without thought and brandy always did that for him.

He mixed his brandy in a decanter. She had found it for him in an antique mall. It was sturdy glass with a schooner etched on it. There was a long neck with a heavy glass ball-topped lid. It was wide and squatty at the bottom, and he felt confident there was a name for the shape, but that did not matter to him. He wasn't going to invite anyone in to see it.

He mixed different types of brandy, in this case, a regular VSOP and a peach-flavored brandy. Slightly more VSOP than peach gave the flavor he liked the best. His decanter came with four glasses with similar schooners etched on them. He poured his brandy up to the second sail on the schooner and walked out to the deck.

There were two chairs made by a Mennonite carpenter with a shop in central Georgia. The chairs swiveled, rocked, and had ottomans that rocked as well. She had bought cushions for them both and had positioned them perfectly to watch the moon rise or to enjoy the changing tides.

He sat there drinking his brandy while on the phone with his kids. He told them about the crazy people at the restaurant and the bartender who amazingly remembered them. They would all be down there in a few weeks for Thanksgiving. This would be his first Thanksgiving on the island without her.

After two or three or four glasses, he went into the house, sat in his recliner, and turned on the TV. This time, he muted it. This was something new for him. He had always slept in as complete darkness as he could create. The only sound, other than the sound of the ocean, was a box fan. He had kept one of those in his room since he moved out of his parent's house when he was nineteen.

He closed his eyes, hoping sleep would come quickly and peacefully, and it did. When the alarm went off at five-thirty like it did every weekday for the past thirty or so years, he was usually waking anyway. He turned the alarm off before walking to the dryer. There was that damn outfit, but at least it was clean and dry since he remembered to turn the dryer on yesterday after he washed it. This was a punishment he had handed down to himself; this outfit at sunrise every day for a year to apologize to her unless it was raining. Even his penance had limits. He was not a flagellant after all.

Chapter 4

She had left in such a hurry that she had forgotten her purse and the keys to her condo. She was halfway up Jones Avenue when she remembered. Angrily, she turned her bike around and pedaled back to get her things.

"Welcome back," Chuck said when he saw her come back into the dining area. "Forget something?" he asked as he held up her purse.

"Thanks," she said.

"Also, here's this," as he handed her a one-hundred-dollar bill. "The guy who pissed you off left this for you."

Pam walked up and asked if she still needed to go home.

"I'm better now, just had to get out of here for a few minutes."

Let's go to my office, Pam said, which in the past had been a washroom or fish cleaning station. "What happened?" asked Pam as they both sat down.

The events were explained just as the customer had related. She thought something was wrong with the food while asking him without thinking about why half his meal was still there.

"It hit me all at once. I realized his wife was dead, and he had simply ordered their meal as they had always done. Then all the memories of Nate came rushing back, overwhelming me with emotion, and I just had to go. Sorry I ran out in the middle of dinner," she apologized.

"Don't worry about it honey," Pam smiled. "We got this covered."

Pam reached into her desk and grabbed a bottle of tequila and a couple of shot glasses. Employees were never allowed to drink while working. Pam explained as she filled the shot glasses that there were exceptions to every rule, and when you are the boss, you can decide whenever an exception needs to be made.

After they finished their shots, Pam hugged her, explaining she was like the daughter she never had. "You can always come to me with anything, honey," she said, smiling.

The rest of the shift was routine.

On the way home, there was a stop at a convenience store for a bottle of cabernet. Tonight, she would let herself relax. Tomorrow was a day off and besides, it was Columbus Day as well as her anniversary.

She opened the bottle after setting her things down and poured a glass since the wine tasted better at room temperature. Then it was off with the bra and clothes and into a warm bath. When she got out of the tub, it was her baggy pink pajama pants with an old Georgia Southern Eagles t-shirt that had belonged to Nate–the only piece of his clothing that she had kept.

The moon would be coming up soon, so she decided to wait for a while, enjoying the moonrise rather than her annual routine of reading the letter.

Tonight was different from the other moonrises. The moon was full and as it reflected off the ocean, it looked like millions of bright neon fish were jumping. For a while, she forgot about everything, enjoying this display of incredible beauty. It was a passing cloud that interrupted the display. She got up to refill her glass and then retrieved the letter from her dresser.

The love of my life,

As I am writing this letter, you are sleeping so peacefully. I am sitting on the balcony with thoughts about our lives together and the joy and happiness we have shared for many years. The ocean is incredible tonight, and I almost came to wake you to see this. The reflection of the moon on the waves is giving off a shimmer like so many sparkling diamonds. I have never seen this before. I must force myself to look away to write this letter to you.

It is my prayer that I can visit my father and destroy this letter as I have twice before. If you are reading this letter, then I am no longer with you. Press this letter against your lips. There is a kiss I left on here for you. My last.

Many times, I have tried to imagine what my life would have been like without you. There is nothing about me that has not been changed and improved because of you in my life. The way you constantly move around, falling asleep if you are still for more than five minutes, the way you tear off pieces of your doughnut instead of biting it, the absolutely ridiculous way you make coffee measuring out the sugar and cream, and the way you hold my hand whenever we are walking together.

Tomorrow is our ninth anniversary and I have to be apart from you.

When I think about our lives together, I need you to know that I have absolutely no regrets, only that my time was cut short. In so many ways, you, as a part of my life gave me the strength to love you and trust you completely. I would marry you again, and again, and again.

While my life has ended, yours has not. You are still an incredibly beautiful woman with the ability to love and to be loved. Please do not close yourself off from the world and deny yourself the happiness you deserve. Do not drown your pain in addiction or isolate yourself from a life of happiness.

In my lifetime, any man who tried to come between you and me would not have cared much for his life. But my life is over. The thought of you alone brings me to absolute despair. I want you to find a man who is not only worthy of your love but who will love you unconditionally for the rest of your life. Just know that I have loved you since the day I met you and am offering you my blessing to move on with your life.

I have two requests: sell my old truck, the title is in the glove box, and buy something for yourself that you don't think you should have. And finally, after you read this letter, please burn it, knowing that a letter can only tie you to the past and can never replace what was lost.

There are no words.

My wife, my lover, my friend

XOXO

She closed her eyes, holding the letter against her lips just as she had done after every reading.

The small handbag she carried every day was the present she bought. A Prada. She had not been able to burn the letter as he requested, nor had she been able to move on. Find someone new, how? She had only ever been on a date with one person. She was certain that she had married her soul mate and lost him. There would never be another Nate or any man who could even come close. Nate was kind, considerate, affectionate, the other half of her and they had never had an argument of any significance or went to bed without telling each other they loved each other while kissing good night.

Whether it was the beautiful night, the view of the ocean, the wine, or a combination of all those things influenced by the events of the day, she fell asleep in the chair with her last thoughts being of him and kissing him goodnight.

Suddenly, she stirred in the chair at the sound of Nate loudly calling her name. It was then she noticed her wine glass broken on the floor. Something was amiss.

The letter was gone.

She checked her chair and the floor, and looked over the balcony—nothing. It was sunrise and as she was peering over the balcony to look at the grass, then out to the dunes, then further out to the beach, she saw nothing. Nothing except that same bastard who had been there yesterday. She rarely confronted anyone about anything and her emotions this morning came as a bit of a surprise to her as well. She was certain of one thing, this person, whoever he was, had come between her and well, she wasn't sure what it was, but she needed to yell at someone, and it was going to be him.

Chapter 5

He had come back to the island on Labor Day and every day, save one during a morning storm, he had stood in this same spot at the same time, serving his penance. Today was just another beautiful sunrise and the feel of fall approaching lingered in the air. Suddenly, he was aware of someone coming up on him from behind. He stepped towards the ocean, both to give himself some space and a bit of time to square up and confront this aggressor.

His sudden movement surprised her, and she was surprised as he turned to face her.

"Stop!" He commanded. Then as quickly, he turned back toward the rising sun.

"I've got something to say to you," she said.

Before she finished talking, he sternly replied, "Two minutes."

She stopped, looking at him as he watched the sun rise until it cleared the horizon.

He turned and said, "Ok, whaddya got to say, crazy lady."

His reply completely disarmed her. She was the sanest person she knew, and *damn.* This was the guy from the restaurant. No words would come out, she just stood there totally dumbfounded.

"This is the shortest conversation I've ever had with a crazy person," he stated. I thought you had something to say.

"Why?" She asked.

"Why what?" He replied.

"Why have you been standing here these past two mornings?" She asked.

"Well, just so you know, I have been in this same spot every day but one since Labor Day, and what business is it of yours?" He replied.

Labor Day? Did I just say that under my breath, out loud? She was thinking.

"Yes," he replied. "Since Labor Day. Why is my being here a problem for you?"

"It's only..." She paused since she could not get the words or her thoughts to stop conflicting. He was the guy interrupting her solitude and he was the sad guy from the restaurant.

"It's only what?" He asked.

"You are not who I expected you to be," she said.

"And exactly who were you expecting me to be, and what is your name, so I don't have to keep calling you crazy lady?"

"Yvonne. And I did not expect the guy in the eighteenth-century pajamas to be the guy from the restaurant."

He had forgotten about his clothes and her comment sent blood rushing to his face. He felt uncomfortable and quickly broke the awkwardness, "Okay then, I'm him and my name is Henry."

Yvonne saw his embarrassed expression and reached out to shake his hand. There was something about his touch that she did not expect, a controlled strength that was present and immediately set her at ease.

She smiled as he took her hand, and he smiled in return.

"Are you hungry?" he asked.

This question was completely unexpected, and she said yes without thinking. *How was he doing this, totally disarming her, and making her feel–that was it exactly–he was making her feel like a person.*

"I can't she said, I'm not dressed, and I'm not wearing any shoes. Haven't showered or anything either. I must look like a crazy lady."

He looked at her and said, "Well, your beige Prada doesn't go with your pink pajamas or your blue shirt, but my house is just down the beach and my wife… he stopped and took a deep breath, doesn't allow shoes on the floor anyway."

"I'm sorry," Yvonne said, surprised that he knew her designer bag.

"It's not your fault. It's just that I haven't had any morning conversation in a while. Anyway, I would like you to have breakfast with me. I don't like eating alone, please join me," he begged.

She agreed to join him, thinking a man had not cooked breakfast for her since her father. Nate was not a cook so when they did have breakfast together, it was usually at Waffle House.

She felt comfortable enough to ask him what he threw in the water yesterday.

He had to think for a moment and was a bit surprised that she had asked him. "It was a watch. Why?"

"Well, yesterday, you were standing so still that at first, I did not see you and it was the sudden throwing motion that caught my eye, but from the distance, I could not see what it was. If you don't mind another question, why did you throw it?"

"Well, until this year, I was a teacher and a coach, and that watch was the one I bought years ago. The clasp was worn out and constantly coming loose so yesterday seemed like a good time to rid myself of it."

"Oh," she commented.

"I have a question for you too. What is so special about today that you were coming down to the beach to give me a piece of your mind?" Henry asked.

She tried to steady her voice, but it trailed off as she said, "It's my anniversary."

There was no more conversation until they reached his house. As they climbed the stairs to the deck, she looked around before saying, "What a beautiful home."

"Thank you." He replied.

The deck ran the length of the house, and the entire front wall was floor-to-ceiling glass. The only exception was at the left end of the deck, which had an outside shower. Screens covered the waterfront side but it was open on the side facing the deck. There were chairs, a table, and an awning that could be extended to provide shade.

They washed off their feet and he had towels in a cabinet on the wall next to the shower. As they entered the house, she saw an incredible kitchen on the left while the rest of the room was open with a corner fireplace.

In the center was a hall that led to two bedrooms and a staircase going up to the roof. He took her to the room on the left which connected to the kitchen. He said, "There is a bathroom in there and you are welcome to shower or bathe. I think you'll find everything you need. I'll be out shortly. These jammies have got to go." Then, he disappeared into the other bedroom before she could think of what to say.

She had never been alone in another man's house and as she opened the door to the bedroom, she saw it was immaculate. *This must be the master bedroom,* she thought, with everything looking as if it had been staged that morning. The king-sized bed was not made but dressed, with ruffles, shams, and throw pillows. The sliding doors led to a small balcony with a wrought-iron bistro set. There was no door, but an entryway to a master bath with the tub of her dreams. It was a claw-foot tub with a sloping back. On either side of the entry to the bathroom were closets, his and hers, with what was obviously hers on the right. Many of her clothes, shoes, and handbags were still there.

Immediately, she thought this was a mistake and started to leave, but she did not know why she stopped. Perhaps it was because she felt safe in a way that she had not felt in a while. She decided to use the shower since she did not feel comfortable bathing in another woman's tub. Much to her surprise, the warm water did not smell like sulfur the way hers did in the condo. The change felt nice and it was refreshing to wash off the remnants of the night and morning.

When she emerged from the bedroom, a towel was wrapped around her head. He thought she looked simply amazing.

"You can have whatever you would like for breakfast as long as it is a bacon, egg, and tomato sandwich," he said with a smile.

She had never experienced eggs in the place of lettuce on a BLT, but it sounded good, so she nodded graciously.

"I've got milk, orange juice, water, or beer," he said.

"Orange juice will do nicely, thank you."

"Do you like mayo and your bread toasted?" He asked.

"Yes, and yes," was her reply. "And by the way, your water doesn't stink. How come?" she asked.

"That was the one thing about the coast I didn't like," he explained. "I thought I would have to live with it but an expensive filtration system did the trick."

As they sat down to eat breakfast, she noticed his left hand start towards her and return. Then, he bowed his head and said his prayer.

When he was finished, she asked why he flinched before praying.

"I always held my wife's hand, and it is reflexive I guess," he replied.

They were quiet during the rest of breakfast, and she was surprised at how good the sandwich tasted. "Thank you for breakfast," she said.

"You're welcome," he replied. "It is nice to share a meal with someone."

As soon as they were finished, he got up, rinsed off the dishes, and put them in the dishwasher.

Wow, this guy was professionally trained, she thought.

He told her, "Under the vanity on the left is a hair dryer and other stuff if you would like to fix your hair."

She said "thanks" as she walked to the bathroom. When she returned, he was sitting facing the TV, which was turned on but muted. He invited her to sit for a while.

When she sat down, he asked, "What happened to your husband?"

Much to her amazement, she was able to speak about Nate, explaining the entire story. Then, she continued and told him about her dream, seeing him on the beach the previous day and how her letter was gone this morning.

"Ten years, wow. I can't imagine what you've been through."

She had heard sympathetic comments from other people and despised sympathy, but she could hear and feel the empathy in his voice. He understood.

"What happened to your wife? If you don't mind me asking."

Before he could say anything, his phone chirped. It was a text from his daughter. He was already standing up when he said, "I've got to go, my daughter has run out of gas on Presidential Parkway."

"Let me give you a ride back to your condo," he added.

She thanked him and started towards the door.

He started for the kitchen. There was a indent in the wall where he kept his keys and wallet. "Ready to go now," he said as he collected them. "But you are going the wrong way."

He motioned for her to follow him down the hall, where another door opened to an elevator. "Come on in," he invited.

The elevator floor was only four feet by four feet, and she felt a little claustrophobic but was interested to see where it went. In about four seconds, the elevator stopped and there was another door that opened to a two-car garage. Directly in front of her was a nice Mercedes convertible. As she stepped into the garage, she froze.

There was an old blue-short-bed Chevy parked beside the Mercedes.

"Sorry about the old truck," he said. "I have to get my gas can and my little sporty car ain't suited for this."

"Where did you get this truck?" She asked.

"About ten years ago, a guy I coached football with, Oliver I think, had bought it and when he came into money a few months later, was going to trade it in. They offered him two thousand and I offered him twenty-five hundred. I needed an old truck to work on this place and it was perfect. Why do you ask?"

She was reaching for the door handle when he reached out and lightly smacked her hand. "Sorry," he said and opened the door for her. "I'm sorry I hit you, I just never let a woman open her door. Not that you aren't capable or anything, it's just..." He stopped talking and closed her door.

He got in and pushed the garage opener before starting the engine.

"My husband had a truck identical to this one," she said. "Except the window handle on this side was broken."

"Well, it was broken when I bought it, but I replaced that handle years ago." Realizing what he had just said and the meaning of it to her, he stopped. "We can go in the other car..."

"No," she interrupted. "This will do fine. I have missed this truck," she said, as a tear streamed down her cheek.

Henry didn't know what to do, so he offered her tissues he kept in the glove box.

Neither spoke as they went up Butler Avenue until they approached her complex. She handed him her gate key and told him to stay to the right as they went around the pools.

"Right here, the end unit on the third floor," she pointed.

Before she could get out, he asked her if she had dinner plans.

While she was thinking of an excuse to say no, Henry said, "I haven't answered your question. I'll answer over dinner."

"What question?" She had forgotten about asking a question.

"What happened to my wife," he spoke. "I'll pick you up at seven, we can even go Dutch if that makes it easier for you."

She had not heard that expression in quite a while and in the absence of any excuse, she simply said "OK."

He handed her his phone and said he would call when he got to the gate. She put her number in and got out.

"Thanks for the breakfast and everything," she said.

"You're welcome." Her phone was ringing, and she realized he was calling. "Just making sure it really was your number," he smiled.

She turned, climbed the stairs, and as she opened the door, she looked back at the parking lot. He waved and drove off.

Immediately, she regretted giving him her number and tried to think of any reason not to go. She did not want to go. It was her anniversary and she wanted to stay home and, what? Do what? She could not think of a single thing she wanted to do.

Henry was pulling up to his daughter's car when his phone chirped. The text was short, 'I can't make it tonight.'

Damn! He thought. *Just damn.*

Chapter 6

Yvonne didn't know why she had just done that. Henry was the nicest person she had met since the people she worked with at the restaurant. It was only then that she looked in the mirror in her bathroom. She realized her hair was a mess, with no makeup, no bra, no panties, barefoot–just a hot mess. How in the world could he have offered to take her to dinner when she looked like this? Another thought came to her as she was looking in the mirror. During the entire morning, dressed like this, he had not been forward with her or ogled her as some of her customers did. Not once had she caught him staring at her chest or body.

She tried to stop thinking about this guy she had just met but she kept wondering what happened to his wife. Well, she knew where he would be in the morning.

Tuesday morning brought rain. A tropical system had stalled just north of Jacksonville and the weather forecasted rain and storms all week. She would stop on her way home from work at the Charles Johnson VA facility today and get some things for the fridge. The causeway to the island would often get covered by heavy rains at high tide and she didn't want to get shut in with no food. It was a good thing she got off a little early because the grocery store was packed. She had picked up the last gallon of water and the bread aisle was skimpy too. The rest of her list was frozen dinners, soups, wine, and an extra bottle just in case.

Wednesday was worse.

Thursday, the causeway flooded, and traffic was stopped in or out of the island.

On Friday, the storm was directly east of the island and the waves were as fierce as she had ever seen. There was flooding on the island, but no one had evacuated. This was not a hurricane, just a strong tropical system. The rain was pounding on her balcony, and she had lost her TV signal two days before.

Saturday, the weather was calmer, but it rained until early afternoon. She had pedaled to the restaurant just to get out of the house and Pam was there, checking for any damage.

Yvonne asked if she could just sit on the deck until sunset.

Pam said, "Sure honey. I'll even sit with you if you want me to."

"Thanks, I've been cooped up for days and it just feels good to see the sun again," said Yvonne.

Pam went towards the bar, yelling back at Yvonne, "You want something to drink, honey?"

Yvonne thought for a minute and said, "a glass of tea, please." She had drunk both bottles of wine this week which was more than she usually drank in a month.

Pam came back with a glass of tea and a large margarita she had prepared for herself, relieved that there was no damage to the deck.

"Here, honey," Pam said as she sat down taking her first sip of the drink. Damn, she loved tequila.

It was about thirty minutes to sunset and after the storm, anyone who even remotely enjoyed sunsets would be watching this one. The colors were already beginning to form. This was going to be an orange darkening to blood red, then to purple, and finally black.

Yvonne was admiring the calmness of the marshes and the live oaks for weathering so many storms over the years. As the sun finished sinking over Savannah and the red sky was darkening to purple, a thought came to her. Henry would be on the beach tomorrow. She smiled at the idea that her life could get back to some sense of normalcy. The first part of October and her anniversary were always the most difficult for her. Now it was over, just like the storm.

As she peddled up Chatham Avenue, the thought of just stopping by his home crossed her mind, but what would she say, and it was getting late. An apology for breaking the dinner engagement is exactly what she would say. As she turned onto Jones Avenue, she decided that she would meet him on the beach in the morning.

Henry was in a lounge chair on the roof of his house. There were two loungers on the roof with a small drink stand between them. The other lounger was empty but, the stand had a bottle of bourbon, a container of ice, and a forty-five automatic on it. He had left the front door unlocked so that in a day or two, when his kids could not get him on the phone, the local police would conduct a welfare check and find him. The mess would be easy to clean up.

During the storm, he left the island to spend a couple of days with his daughter and son. Two days at each house were all he could normally last, not that he did not love his kids, or that their spouses were intolerable, but he liked sleeping in his own bed; or since she died in the recliner.

News from his son had sent him into a spiral he was not sure he could manage. Next year, he was going to be a grandfather. He was happy, not as happy as his son and daughter-in-law, and not as happy as he would otherwise have been because his happiness was tempered by the knowledge that his wife would have been soaring above the clouds. She had so badly wanted to be a grandmother to do all that baby stuff again. The thoughts of a grandbaby without a grandma, grandmother, nana, nina, or whatever the little squigdigit could say was pure torture.

The sunset had been truly magnificent. Now that darkness was settling in, he thought he was ready to end his pain and suffering. Only one thing was stopping him. He had made a vow, to be at the spot at sunrise for a year and he still had ten months to go. Why this vow was so important to him was beyond his ability to reason right now. More painful was the knowledge that he had broken a vow before.

They had only been married for a little over two years and he was in his senior year at the University of Georgia. The Ranger battalion at UGA had a little rental house that the brothers over the years had passed down from one class to the other. The brothers renting the house were having a party, celebrating something he could not remember, but he and his wife had gone that night. The music in the house was loud, so she stayed outside talking to a group of his friends and wishing they could leave.

He had asked for a few more minutes. Then he had gone into the house to find a restroom. A girl from the ROTC unit had seen him coming out of the restroom and blocked his path, saying she had something to tell him in private. After they closed the door, she unzipped her dress, dropping it to the floor. Nothing like this had ever happened to him before. He had read about it in magazines, or it happened in pornographic movies, but there she was, and she was unzipping his pants. She was telling him something without speaking and his reply would be very acceptable to her, at least that is what he took from her moans.

The most difficult part of all this was the knowledge his wife was prettier, had a better body, and was a tigress in bed.

When his wife asked him, what took so long? His reply was the only lie he ever told her.

"I had to shit," he said.

Henry was sure the lie was transparent, and his face was telling the truth.

She knew he had an anxiety issue, and his movements could be sudden so she accepted his answer without consideration and simply said, "Can we go now?"

As far as he knew, the only other person who knew of this indiscretion never spoke of it or possibly didn't even remember it. But he did. And the knowledge of that betrayal haunted him and would continue to haunt him for the rest of his life. Surrendering his integrity on an impulse had led to his outbursts over the years, his overprotectiveness of his wife, as well as his anger whenever her expression showed any level of disappointment.

No, he would not kill himself until the year had passed, and he had fulfilled every day of this vow.

Chapter 7

Yvonne had set her alarm clock to be sure she would be awake at sunrise. Today, she did not want to look as wrecked as she had been when they first met. Today, she would have her makeup on, a conservative one-piece black bathing suit with a white mesh sundress over everything. She had lost track of time a bit by thinking about her morning with Henry the previous week, particularly at how together he seemed for someone who recently had lost his wife. She had decided during the week that at the minimum, he was someone who could be a friend.

She had called her old friend Karen, back in Statesboro, to talk to her about Henry. Of all the people she had been friends with while Nate was alive, Karen was the only person who talked to her the way she had before he died.

Karen asked so many questions for which she had no answers. She had also asked what Yvonne would do if he wanted to be more than friends. She had laughed when she told Karen she did not know, but when they shook hands and later when he had smacked her hand for reaching for the door handle on the truck, his touch had seemed very measured and controlled. Yvonne also told her that he also had a fierce look when he was angry or upset which made her apprehensive about his temperament.

Karen was always direct, outspoken, and sometimes vulgar. Her next question was about his 'package.'

Yvonne had laughed as she told her she had no idea. They had only met twice, once he was sitting and the other, they were walking together, but she would tell her if she found out.

Yvonne grabbed her bag, shut the door, and headed directly out to the beach. "NO!" She yelled. The sun had just cleared the horizon and Henry was leaving. She kicked her sandals off because she was going to have to jog to catch him. As she started jogging, to her dismay, so did he.

Henry had enjoyed this sunrise. His melancholic thoughts of the night before had passed with the night, allowing thoughts of the upcoming birth of a grandchild to cheer him. All the days being cooped up by the storm had left him feeling restless and a good jog this morning had already helped. He had jogged to their spot on the beach with a return trip being just what he needed to get his muscles loose and his blood pumping.

He did not see her emerging from the dunes as he turned to run to his house.

Immediately, Yvonne stopped. There was no way she could catch him and if she ran the whole way to his house, her makeup as well as any attempt to look attractive would be wasted. She returned to the bicycle rack in front of the condo and started pedaling. If she pedaled too fast, the same effect as running would result so she decided that he wasn't running that fast and if she pedaled at a normal speed, they would arrive at about the same time. She was wrong.

Henry had sprinted the last quarter mile to his house. His clothes quickly came off and he laid them over one of the chairs, then headed to the shower. This morning, he received a special gift on his way home. Of all the seabirds he loved, seagulls were not on that list. Most birds had an order that appealed to him. Pelicans flew in formations, albatrosses were solitary, and herons were just beautiful but, the characteristic they all had in common was that they stayed away from people. It was a group of seagulls foraging near a garbage can that gave him his gift. One of those bastards had dropped a shit bomb that landed right on the top of his head. He had never seen it coming. When it hit him, he immediately reached up to see what it was, and it smeared on his hand.

He was washing his hair when Yvonne came up the stairs and he did not know she was there.

Yvonne heard the shower as she came up the stairs and thought he was washing his feet as they had done the week before. As she walked towards the shower, she could see him standing there. He was not washing his feet.

To say she was shocked was the understatement of the year. Her stare only lasted a couple of seconds but, so many thoughts went through her head. He was muscular, not like a bodybuilder but like an MMA fighter before they cut weight to fight. She had watched hundreds of fights with her father so she knew that if Henry had been a fighter this would be his training weight. *About two hundred and twenty to thirty pounds,* she thought. That thought lasted about a millisecond because she could also see the 'package' Karen had asked about. Karen had a quarter horse, a gelding that she rode as a barrel racer. She had named him Naughty Boy because for whatever reason, he would often extend his penis from its sheath. Not that he could do anything with it though.

Henry immediately reminded her of Naughty Boy.

She saw his hands begin to wipe his eyes, so she quickly turned away and mumbled, "Sorry."

He opened his eyes and for the briefest of moments, he thought his wife was standing there.

"Hi," he said, reaching for a towel. "Wasn't expecting anyone to be here this morning."

To Yvonne's surprise, he did not rush to cover himself. He toweled off as he had done thousands of times and then wrapped the towel around his waist. Not that the towel did much. The bulging outline of his penis was still very visible against the white towel.

"I wanted to tell you I was sorry," she said.

"You just did," Henry replied.

"Not for seeing you naked, I'm not sorry about that." *Wait, that's not what I meant to say*, she thought. "No, what I meant to say was I came to apologize for missing dinner last week."

While she was stumbling over her words, Henry just smiled, asking if she wanted to come in. He would make breakfast after he showered and shaved. He said as he opened the door for her, "You look great today, and your bag doesn't clash with your outfit."

She said "thanks" as he walked in behind her. She was wrong when she thought he had not looked at her though.

He knew way more than she realized. She was five feet four inches tall, and one hundred and thirty pounds, give or take a few. A full thirty-four 'C' or perhaps 'D,' and her ass was perfect. He never liked women who were skin and bones but, rather a little on the curvy side. She could also spend a little time in the sun since her skin was a little paler than he thought it should be. Her brunette hair was perfect but, there was about a one-inch strip of white hair on the left side of her forehead. He had heard an old wives' tale about those patches of white hair that were caused by an angel's kiss.

His wife had looked very much like Yvonne when she was younger but, with slightly smaller breasts, and shorter hair. She had been a dark brunette, almost black, and as she had begun to age, it turned a beautiful platinum color that looked like she had dark undertones. For years, he had begged her to 'let it go' and once she did, she often got asked 'Who does your hair' or 'Where did you get that done.' Almost no one believed her when she said this was her natural color. It helped that Henry had changed her name on his phone and began to call her his Platinum Goddess. That is how she remained for the rest of her life.

Henry got out of the shower with the noticeable aroma of bacon coming from the kitchen. Yvonne had started breakfast.

"You don't have to do that," Henry said as he emerged from the guest bedroom. He had not been able to go in the master bedroom or bathroom since his wife died, except to clean and dust. She was everywhere in that room and nowhere at the same time. As he rounded the island to where Yvonne was standing, he smiled and said he was going to have to work extremely hard to control himself.

Yvonne, with a concerned look, asked him what he meant.

"Well, I'm kind of a control freak so whenever my wife and I were in here together usually I would re-scramble the eggs, take over the bacon frying, slice the tomatoes, relegating her to the toast."

"Oh," she said as her concerns were alleviated.

"And one other thing," he said. "If you stand in front of the sink, my instincts would be to grab your ass and kiss your neck."

"Then I'll avoid the sink," she said, although, she did not consider it a deal breaker.

"That is exactly what my wife said she always tried to do. Her neck was irresistible but, more importantly, it got her blood to boil, so she would shoo me away to finish the dishes."

"What was her name?"

"Virginia," he said looking away from the kitchen.

"Do you need any help with anything," he asked.

She said, "No, just sit down; I'll finish making these sandwiches."

Sitting the plates down she turned to get their drinks, milk, and orange juice.

When Yvonne sat down, she held her right hand out toward him.

Henry reached out, holding her hand by the fingers the way a sovereign or bishop would allow their hand to be touched for fealty.

As his short prayer ended, she tried to pull her hand back but there was no escape from his grasp. Instead, she watched as he pulled her hand slightly closer to him while bringing his lips to her fingers.

How can a man who looks like him be this kind and gentle she thought?

"That was sweet," she said.

"Well, you offered your hand and that is what I do," he replied.

She decided if she were around him at mealtime, he could always hold her hand.

When they finished, Henry said that his breakfast was much better than when he had prepared it, while he quickly took the dishes to the sink to rinse them.

Yvonne thought she would move quicker next time to see if his threats about the sink were true.

"What made it better?" Yvonne asked.

"You made it for me," was his reply. "Food someone else makes for you is always better than the food you make for yourself."

His words felt like a warm blanket or a soothing bath. Breakfast seemed like such a trivial thing to warrant anyone's contemplations.

"How did you meet?" She asked as they sat in the living room.

Henry took a deep breath, and leaned back in his chair. "In a church," he said. "I had recently been discharged from the Army…"

"You were in the military?" She interrupted.

"…Yes, I was in the 1st Battalion of the 325th Parachute Infantry Regiment," he said.

"We were stationed at Ft. Bragg too," she interrupted again.

"Anyway," he continued… She could see he was a bit annoyed at the interruptions when he was trying to answer a question. He would rather not talk about, so she decided not to interrupt again.

"I was going to school at Gordon Junior College…"

So badly she wanted to interrupt to say she thought he graduated from the University of Georgia since she could see the diploma but, she held back.

"…living at home in my old room, in my old bed, and attending church where my father pastored. One Sunday in mid-August, we were having a homecoming with a meal after the service. I did not see her come into the church. She came with a school friend so they could enjoy dinner. Sometime in the past, she had attended there when her grandfather was a minister at this church."

When the service ended, I could hear giggling behind me and as I turned, I saw her. Those ice-blue eyes and short dark hair caught my attention. This old busybody who was a member of the church named Mrs. Whatley tried to play matchmaker, escorting the three of us to a Sunday school class so we could, as she put it, get acquainted.

"That is so nice," Yvonne said. "What a sweet thing for her to do."

"Do you have any pictures?" Yvonne asked.

Now that question had pierced him. She noticed a painful expression on his face. She had only asked because the walls were decorated as if a realtor was showing the house there was nothing personal anywhere.

"Yes," he said. "I put them all in here." He walked towards the hall to the guest bedroom.

As she walked by the buffet where he kept his beverages, she noticed something she had not seen before–the forty-five automatic.

He opened the door and said have a look.

When she entered, there were pictures everywhere, dating from when they were first married to ones that had to be just before she had died. Every picture had the same pose, his arm around her with both of her arms around him and her head firmly affixed to his chest. The photos were from all over the United States. They had traveled quite a bit.

Well, she thought she was a stay-at-home wife. He was a teacher with the summer off. Yvonne did not know much about high school football. In Georgia, there is no such thing as a summer off.

While she and his wife were similar in terms of hair color, and overall body type, facially they did not look alike at all. His wife's teeth were perfectly even while Yvonne's two front teeth were slightly longer than the others. His wife's eyes were the color of an Alaskan glacier, while Yvonne's eyes were an ordinary shade of brown.

The younger pictures of his wife did remind her of someone. She could have been the twin sister of her red-haired, green-eyed friend Karen. Their facial features were eerily similar, but Karen was five feet seven inches and had incredibly long legs.

"What did you think?" he said, as she walked out of the room.

"She was beautiful," said Yvonne. "What happened to her?"

"I promised I would tell you but not right now. I've got to meet an old coaching buddy soon to help him move a refrigerator since he doesn't have a truck. Let me take you home since you are on the way, tonight you can come back for the dinner we didn't get to have. These conversations are much easier in the evening with some libations."

"I can't," she said. "An old friend is coming by tonight. Why don't you come to my house, and I'll cook dinner for you?"

"Love to. What are we having? Asked Henry.

"Baked cod and salad," she responded.

The word love was spoken so easily unlike the pained way most men say it if they say it at all. He was not afraid of the word and that made her feel even more comfortable around him.

"I've got my bike anyway, so you don't have to bother," she replied.

"Not going to happen," he said with a smile.

They gathered their things, this time going out the front door since her bike was parked at the stairs to his deck.

As they walked out the door, she glanced over at the shower, remembering exactly how he had looked a couple of hours ago. Her decision was made. If he wanted to be more than just friends, she would only offer encouragement. She was not sure what his intentions were since he was difficult to figure out, usually surprising her. He had been married a long time though. If her heart was still mending what must he be going through? She had been married for nine years and a widow for ten, he had been married almost as long as she had been on the earth.

He pushed the bike to the garage, placing it in the bed of his truck, then reached for the handle to his door. Yvonne was standing beside the door exactly the way his wife used to stand while waiting for him to perform his duty. Quickly, he hurried to her side of the truck where she was smiling, really smiling, like he had not seen before. *She is a beautiful woman,* he thought, but perhaps too young for him.

Here, he held out his hand.

"For what?" She asked.

"Smack it," Henry said. "That is the punishment for forgetting."

She lightly tapped his hand and they both smiled while he performed his duty of opening her door.

Again, he waited until she was in her condo before leaving. She immediately changed into some comfy clothes to clean the place before Karen or Henry arrived. Neither of them would be there for several hours so when she finished, she went to have a bath.

Relaxing in a tub was one of her favorite things to do. Usually, her mind was blank but now all she could think about was Henry in that shower. She reached down to pleasure herself while wishing all the while it was his hand instead, or something else providing her pleasure. The orgasm was nice but, unlike other times, this one left her wanting more, much more. It left her wanting a man–not just any man–she wanted Henry. As she was picking out which dress she was going to wear over her sexiest black lace panties, a dreadful thought occurred to her. If Karen were there, Henry would be distracted by her, or even worse, attracted to her. She did resemble his wife with her long red hair and legs. Karen had been through a few men in her life but never married. She said men were like shoes, fun to shop for, wear a couple of times, then move on. She was thinking of a way to keep her away from dinner and Henry that night when she heard a knock on her door.

It was Karen.

Karen was wearing a pair of black yoga pants and a loose-fitting white, sleeveless top with a collar. She looked like she just stepped out of a catalog. *Damn!* thought Yvonne, *how could she compete with this?*

Karen said, "Hey girl! How ya doing?" as she put her arms around Yvonne for a hug. "Haven't seen you in a while. You look different. What's up?"

Yvonne told her the events of the day but left out details–one big detail in particular. She also explained Henry would be joining them later for dinner. "Great," said Karen. "I've never had Silver Fox before, I usually like them younger with more stamina. I'm eager to see what this old guy looks like."

Yvonne bristled at that but, only on the inside. Outside, she forced a smile while thinking all the while that Karen better keep her paws off Henry.

Yvonne changed the topic of the conversation to Karen, which was easy. Karen loved to talk about her life and all the things that were going on. They were finishing their first glass of wine, as well as Karen's latest conquest, a Gulf Stream pilot who jetted her to New York for dinner.

Then, there was a knock at the door.

Yvonne opened the door. Henry was standing there dressed in a pair of slacks, a white shirt, a red tie, and a navy jacket. He could not keep the look of surprise off his face.

The little black dress Yvonne was wearing showed her figure in a most flattering manner and he was thinking how good it would look wrinkled on the floor.

He handed her a vase of flowers while he held a bottle of Chardonnay.

"Thank you but, where did you park and why didn't you call," Yvonne asked.

"Well," he embarrassingly replied. "When you canceled, I thought I would never see you again, so I deleted your number. I parked across the street at the convenience store."

"Hellooo," Karen said in a voice that indicated he would be the supper instead of joining them for it. "I'm Karen." She stepped between them and wrapped her arms around Henry, making sure she felt his chest as well as him feeling hers up against him. As she released him, she turned towards Yvonne, saying 'Wow' without any sound.

Yvonne felt the temperature in her face rising, hoping all the while the flush from the wine would hide her anger. *Karen had better get the hint that this was more than a pair of shoes,* she thought. There were no circumstances in which Yvonne was a sharing kind of person.

When Henry asked to use the restroom, Yvonne took the opportunity to let Karen know that there might be a chance at more than a friendship with Henry.

Karen stopped smiling, knowing all that her friend had been through and that her conversations about this man had not included the fact that she was developing feelings for him–feelings she had closed off for a long time. "I'm sorry," Karen said. "Would you like me to leave?"

Yvonne could not believe the words that came out of her mouth so quickly, "Yes, I would," she instantly replied.

Karen grabbed her purse and hugged Yvonne while whispering in her ear, "Get him, girl..."

Karen could never be angry with Yvonne. They had been friends forever; besides, she had a secret she would never tell Yvonne, so the least she could do was give her space. As she walked out the door, she looked back whispering, "...or I will."

When Henry came out of the bathroom, he looked around, asking where Karen was.

Yvonne lied, "She got a text and had to go."

There was a different expression on Yvonne's face that Henry didn't recognize. "Are you okay?" He asked.

Yvonne did not answer his question but asked him if he was hungry.

"Not really," was his answer.

She walked towards him, put her arms around his neck, and asked, "Will you kiss me?"

Chapter 8

Her words were still registering in his brain when he reacted without considering the consequences. His arms immediately embraced her as he leaned down to place his lips against hers. He was in no rush to kiss her. *There could only be one first kiss,* he thought. Carefully, he made sure both of his lips touched her top lip, then down to her bottom lip, and finally, both of their lips were joined together.

Her mouth opened for him while he opened his for hers. The chardonnay was the first thing he noticed when she welcomed his tongue.

The kiss was excellent, Yvonne thought, *but why was he stopping?* She did not want him to stop.

"Before this goes any further," Henry said. "There are things you must know about me."

"I know you," she said.

"How old am I?" He asked. Without waiting for a reply, he continued, "You are an incredibly beautiful young woman with, hopefully, a long life in front of you. The best of my life is behind me, and you have no idea who I am or the baggage that comes along with me."

"I don't care," she said. "I have not met a person who made me feel like living until I met you."

"Okay," he said. "There is nothing I want more and deserve less than to have a woman like you in my life. But before that can happen, you have to know who I am and exactly what you are getting yourself into."

"Alright, let's sit down so you can tell me, she said.

They moved to her sofa, sitting next to each other.

He was not sure where to begin so he asked her, "Do you know why I am at the beach at sunrise every day?"

"You said it was because of the outfit?" She asked.

"That is mostly true he said, but it is more than that. She bought me that outfit for our last vacation before she died," he explained. "And I would not wear it. Virginia loved romance novels, the ones that have a long-haired bodybuilder on the cover with a scantily clad woman. She said I was that for her so she bought the outfit, I tried it on but immediately took it off swearing I would never wear it. While all of that is true, it is not the entire story."

"Yvonne, I am a cheater and a liar," Henry stated, with a sincerity in his voice that made her feel anger towards him, sympathy for Virginia, as well as curiosity for the sudden confession.

Suddenly, he could not look into her condemning eyes, so he looked at the floor.

Yvonne was not sure if she wanted to hear his confession. A cheater and a liar would continue to cheat and lie. Just as she was about to ask him to leave, he continued.

"We were still relatively newlyweds..." he explained, relating the entire story to her. He did not try to make any excuses for his actions, further explaining that the betrayal was an anchor he carried throughout their marriage, a check on his arrogance, anger, and any real criticism of anything she did because it did not equate to his actions.

"Why didn't you tell her?" Yvonne asked.

"I couldn't," Henry explained. "She loved me very much and would have forgiven me. Our lives would have continued except she would have never looked at me the same. It was not right for me to force her to carry the weight of my indiscretion, it was my burden to bear besides, even if she forgave me, I could never and still have not forgiven myself."

"Did it ever happen again," Yvonne asked.

"Never," he said. "For the rest of our marriage. I never allowed myself to be in a situation where the remotest chance of infidelity would even be possible."

"You are the first person I have ever explained this to Yvonne," he stated.

"Why did you tell me?" She asked.

"I wanted you to know the worst thing I ever did so that you would know I am capable of breaking a vow I made before witnesses, God, and the woman I loved. If you want me to leave and never bother you again, I will, or you can ask me any questions you have an interest in knowing the answer to and I will tell you."

"Will you help me cook dinner?" She asked.

Henry smiled, quickly rising to his feet while offering his hand to help her up.

"I thought you were going to ask me to leave," he said with audible relief in his voice.

"I still may, if you ruin the cod," she smiled.

"Then let me prepare the salad so that can't happen," he said, turning the oven to preheat.

While dinner was being prepared, the conversation primarily involved getting-to-know-each other questions. When Yvonne said she was thirty-eight, Henry asked her if a twenty-year age difference was a deal breaker.

Yvonne set the salads on the table. The look on her face was one Henry was sure he would never want to cause.

"I have been dead for ten years," Yvonne said. "The first emotions I've had other than despair, grief, or hopelessness have been since I met you."

Henry was thinking about walking around the peninsula which separated the stove from the table to hug Yvonne when she asked, "Why is my age an issue for you?"

That question hit him like a brick. Suddenly, he was defensive to the point that his only response was honesty. "You are so young and beautiful," he said. "There must be thousands of younger men who have so much more to offer you, including a family..."

Yvonne interrupted him, "I can't have children," she said with a blank expression. "Nate and I tried to conceive. We were both examined by doctors and while he was determined to be normal, the doctors could never tell me why I was not able to have a baby. We really don't know each other."

"I'm so sorry," Henry pleaded. "Never in a million years would I ever intentionally do or say anything to bring you such anguish."

"I didn't mean it to sound that way," she said. "It's just that I am not the kind of woman most men are looking to have a relationship with when they find out I am broken. I am not willing to open myself up to the disappointment in their faces when they realize I am an empty womb."

Henry walked around the peninsula, taking her in his arms and looking into her eyes as if he could see into her very soul.

"Yvonne," he said. "Children are not the purpose of a marriage. Marriage is the joining of a man and a woman to mutually share a life's journey, filling the emptiness each person has from the moment of birth. If children result in that union, their lives can be enriched or torn apart but, they are not the purpose."

This time, he kissed her. His emotions were not inhibited by his past betrayals. She knew the worst about him, and perhaps he knew her secret too. This kiss was long and passionate with their bodies pressed tightly against each other, wishing the contact was skin against skin. When their lips finally separated, she took a deep breath and said with an exhale, "I think the cod is done."

Henry laughed as he walked to the oven. The cod was done, perfectly so, as were the salads. They sat down to enjoy their dinner and she held out her hand.

Henry took it, blessed the food, and kissed her hand before reaching for his fork. *This was an excellent meal,* he thought, prepared not by one person but by two people for each other.

Yvonne wondered if she could get past his past indiscretions, lies, and betrayals. Those mistakes were what made him the man he was. He did not do any of that to her. He had been the most complete gentleman she had ever met, and his manners were impeccable.

As they finished their meal, she quickly reached for the dishes, retreating to the sink to rinse them off.

Henry watched her turn on the faucet, then got up from the table. He walked into the kitchen and as he came up behind her. His fingers brushed her hair away from the right side of her head. His lips found their way to the base of her neck as his hands found the outside of her hips. This time, beside his lips, his teeth bit slightly into her skin while he pressed himself against her.

"I told you this might happen," he said.

If this is what happens after dinner, she thought, *he would never do the dishes again.*

"I've had worse," she almost whispered, then exhaled deeply. The kiss had an audible effect.

When the dishes were finished, they returned to the sofa, continuing their talk about each of their pasts. Each hanging on the stories the other detailed, becoming more attached with each passing word.

Yvonne asked, "What happened to your wife?"

Henry's face lost any expression and he asked, "Do you have anything to drink other than wine?"

"There is bourbon in the cabinet beside the refrigerator," she said.

He instinctively looked in the cabinet above the sink to retrieve a glass, filled it with ice, and then bourbon, asking if she would like one as well. When she said, "no," he took a sip on his way to the sofa.

"We had been renovating our house," he explained, going into detail about the problems with the cabinets, which took until March instead of February to be installed. They had moved in just after the Saint Patrick's Day holidays which was spring break for all the schools in Chatham County. Everything was going perfectly with one exception; their bed was the only furniture they had moved from Wilmington Island to the beach house, but the headboard had cracked when he had to swerve to miss a car that crossed the center line while on the island highway to Tybee. He smiled as he told her the crack was not visible but, during a particularly energetic display of affection one night, the right side of the bed had collapsed to the floor, with both of them rolling out. They had laughed as they hit the floor, but the demise of the bed did not prevent the completion of their affections.

The next day, he supported the bed with wooden blocks and assured her it was okay. Her reaction was that it was time for a new bed, so they began the search. Virginia had wanted the perfect bed for their house so her search would not be quick. He had hoped they could just go pick a bed out at a store and be done with it but, this was going to be their retirement bed.

He had come home from a summer workout with the football team when she met him at the door.

"I've found it," she had said. On the phone was a complete bedroom suite from an expensive store that did not have a showroom in the entire southeast.

They would have to order it, but he could not say no or even calm her enthusiasm. Throughout their marriage, they had only one new bed–the one they broke, and never a complete bedroom set. Being married to a coach meant lots of moves and expensive furniture simply did not make sense.

The bedroom suite had been ordered with a delivery date sometime after the Fourth of July. All the high schools in Georgia have a dead week during the week of the fourth. There can be no athletic activities of any kind so even coaches get time to be with their families. This would be the first year they would get to vacation in their own retirement home–not travel, not fight traffic, no hotel reservations, no children–just them, peaceful and relaxed. That is exactly what the week had been, morning walks on the beach holding hands, lunches at different restaurants, dinners in their house, and evenings on the roof.

The Fourth had been on a Saturday. Their walk at sunrise had been on a Sunday, and he had to go back to work on Monday. It wasn't that much of an imposition on the summer, just a couple of hours from nine to noon on Mondays, Wednesdays, and Thursdays, with an occasional passing tournament in the afternoon thrown in, five to seven tournaments at the most, and a few baseball games.

That Monday, she had awakened feeling a bit under the weather, mostly a headache, which she had complained of having for years so no walk on the beach this morning. Instead, they cooked breakfast and sat on the deck having their morning coffee until it was time for him to leave for practice. It was a running joke between his son and daughter that their mom was the sickest person any of them knew. She had demonstrated, in the past, a knack for developing symptoms of the latest virus, disease, or recent medical malady.

He always called her to let her know he was on his way home. Occasionally, she did not answer so he was often unconcerned but slightly annoyed. He had received an email that their bedroom suite would be delivered the next day. He got off the elevator and was on his way to the shower. "Did you get the email about the furniture, girlfriend," he said as he was opening the door to the bedroom. She was lying on the couch as she always did when she napped. When there was no reply or any response at all, he stopped in the doorway to the bedroom. She was an incredibly light sleeper, the slightest squeak of his recliner being lowered would immediately cause her to stir, so the fact that he had come in from the elevator, talked to her, and opened the bedroom door with no response immediately sent him to her side.

He stopped talking. Tears were streaming down his cheeks.

"I killed her," Henry said.

"How did you kill her?" Yvonne asked.

He told her about the damn dog and what he had said.

"I told her she had to die before me. There was no way I could bear the pain of her being left alone without me or anyone to comfort her," he said. "The way Nate left you."

Every word he had said opened wounds she thought were long since closed but, at the same time, offered some consolation. Her husband had indeed left her to endure the grief, emptiness, and infinite loneliness of being a Gold Star wife.

He got up and poured another drink, without ice this time, and one for Yvonne as well.

"When I put my hand on her arm to wake her, I knew," he said. Dropping to my knee tears came to my eyes much as they are right now, "I was crying out; girlfriend, girlfriend, girlfriend... Virginia, please wake up."

"I don't know how long I knelt there crying, pleading with her, God, or whatever power there was in the universe to come back to me. But I knew she was gone, never to return. What do I do next? How do I tell my brothers and sisters, her parents, our children? Finally,

I picked up my phone to call Colonel Patrick from the VFW."

"Colonel, I said, I need you to help me. He could tell from the tone of my voice because he asked, who is this?"

"It's Lieutenant Morgan," I said. "I don't know what to do."

"Why? Was his answer."

"My wife is dead, was all I could say."

"The call ended. Less than ten minutes later Colonel Patrick was walking through the door from the front deck. He put his arm around me and said 'son, please go sit on the deck.' He made a few calls and then came out to join me with the bottle of bourbon from my bar."

"We didn't use any glasses, just one after another, taking a drink from the bottle. He had been through these many times before from Vietnam through the beginning of the Wars in the Middle East. He had served for thirty-three years, and his face was marked with the scars of countless soldiers who had made the ultimate sacrifice as well as from the faces of family members they left behind."

"The police arrived a few minutes later along with the coroner, EMTs, the fire department, and damn near everyone on the island it seemed. Colonel Patrick stayed until I was finished giving my statement, then he said my children would be at the VFW when I was finished."

"The police officer who took my statement said I should not be driving so he gave me a ride to the VFW. It was seven when I arrived to see my children standing with Colonel Patrick. They knew something was horribly wrong when they saw my face and immediately began to ask where their mom was."

"Telling my son and daughter their mom was dead was the hardest thing I have ever done. Forever, I will be indebted to Colonel Patrick, it was he who called the remaining family members to tell them of my loss."

"It was a beautiful morning two weeks later when a small group of family and friends gathered at the spot where I stand every morning to say our goodbyes. As the sun began to rise, we began the process of scattering her ashes. I went last just as the sun cleared the horizon. The final ashes from her urn were scattered as I muttered, goodbye girlfriend, through my tears. I dropped the urn onto the sand, turning to face my loved ones with a hole in my heart I was sure could never be repaired."

"I'm so sorry," Yvonne said.

Chapter 9

After a pause, he sat up straight, looking her in the eyes, and said, "Let's change the subject but not too far. I'll ask you a question, then you can ask me one. If you chose not to answer, there must be a reason other than I don't want to answer. I'll go first. How long has the white streak been in your hair?"

There were no pictures in the living room, so he was not sure, but imagined it had been there since birth. He was wrong.

"You may not believe this, but I was not born with this patch of white hair. The morning after the officers arrived to tell me my husband was gone, a spot appeared near my scalp, so I just let it grow."

He had immediately regretted that question but it was her turn.

She decided she would ask a simple question about a number, nothing too difficult but rather a pointed question about his life. "How many women have you been with other than your wife?" She asked.

Damn, he thought. *Straight for the jugular.* He thought for a moment, counting on his fingers "Five, no six, kind of," he said, looking puzzled.

"What do you mean kind of?" She said. "Is it five or six?"

"The answer is really embarrassing," he offered. "The only other person who experienced this is who knows where, I've never seen her again."

"Explain," Yvonne demanded.

"Ok." Then he began, "Until I was thirteen years old, I was one of the smallest boys at my school. When puberty began, it was with a boom. In one summer, I went from five feet two inches tall to six feet. When school began in the fall of the eighth grade, I was one of the tallest boys in school, but I only weighed one hundred and thirty pounds, super lanky. Over the next three years, my coordination returned as well as much-needed muscle; then I weighed about one hundred and sixty pounds. I met this girl, whose name I swear I cannot remember, perhaps it is a sort of defensive coping mechanism but, she made it clear to me at our first meeting, that I was the person she would give her virginity to if I had a car. I made it clear to her that I had a car and would pick her up on Friday at eight."

"Where did you meet this girl," Yvonne asked.

"That is also embarrassing." Henry said. "I have an older brother who went to a church with a younger congregation, so I had gone to church with him this particular Sunday."

"In church?" She said laughingly. "Did you meet all your women in a church?"

He stopped her, "Which is another question, so when I finish this horrible telling of the tale of my misfortune, it will be my turn."

She laughed harder at that statement, trying not to humiliate him.

"So, I had the opportunity to ponder the soon-to-be experience all week. Probably, heightened the expectation way more than was necessary," he said.

"Growing up on a farm with a preacher as a father is not the best way to learn about sexuality," he continued. "My sex talk with my father was short and sweet. One of our cows was in estrus so the bull was doing what bulls do. I was about eleven when I asked my father what the bull was doing. Breeding her son, was his reply, we will have a new calf in the fall."

"'How do you know,' I asked. My father was a preacher but, he could also be brutally blunt."

"Because he is sticking his dick in her, son," was his reply.

"That was the first inappropriate word I had ever heard my father use, so it brought an end to my questions."

"The internet did not exist in those days so neither I nor any of my friends had ever seen a pornographic movie, only the pages of men's magazines."

He continued, as Yvonne hung onto every word as if he were telling some great epic of the ancient Greeks or Romans, "When the night arrived, I picked her up in my Volkswagen Beetle."

"A what?" Yvonne now burst out laughing. "You've got to be kidding me."

"'I wish I were," he replied.

"I knew a secluded place near the reservoir where we could be alone to share this experience. Foreplay was a word I had heard before but, to me, it had no meaning. On this evening, foreplay was opening the door, stepping outside, removing your clothes then trying to fit on the back seat of a VW."

Yvonne could see everything he was explaining. Her laughter was increasing now to the point where he had to pause to let her gather herself.

"Glad you are enjoying this," he smiled.

"My shirt came off quickly," he said. "But I was wearing boots. While I turned to sit on the edge of the fender to remove my boots, she was lying on the back seat with one foot on the folded-down driver's seat and the other against the roof of the car. When I stood up and turned around to see her in that position, her perfect brown pubic hair exposed the answer to a young boy's burning questions. The geyser erupted."

Now Yvonne was laughing hysterically. "All over her?" She asked, laughing even more.

"No," was his reply. "I had put on a condom so she had no idea what had just happened to me but, from previous experiences in the bathroom I knew I had to hurry, or the opportunity would be gone. By the time I had contorted myself to get into position, the chance was gone. I spent the next three or four minutes trying to fit my flaccid penis into her virgin vagina."

"Oh my God," said Yvonne through her laughter. "'Kind of' is the correct expression. You must have been humiliated."

"You have no idea, the only saving thing was that she was a virgin too, so I hoped she didn't know the difference."

"Ok Yvonne," he said as her laughter diminished. "Where was your first sexual encounter?"

Her laughter stopped. Yvonne's expression hid any thoughts or emotions. She fixed her gaze directly into his eyes as if she were about to strike him with a blinding universal truth. And her response did.

"On the seat of your truck." She stated.

There was no more explanation, just her eyes fixed on his. His thoughts or his ability to think or reason suddenly left him. She stood up from her seat on the sofa, directly in front of him. She held out her hands for him to grasp and join her. This time, Yvonne put her arms around his neck. Henry put one arm around her body, grabbing her gently by the back of her hair with one hand, tilting her head so her mouth could accept his kiss and finding the upper curves of her shapely ass with the other. The kiss was slow and passionate.

When Yvonne reached to begin to undo his trousers, he quickly grabbed her wrists to stop her.

"Not tonight" he said. "Right now the bourbon is talking, dulling the sensations, and providing excuses for actions we might regret later. I don't want anything to dampen one moment, one sensation, or the pleasure of a single kiss. I want to take you to bed Yvonne, but not tonight."

"Okay," she said. She was surprised by his restraint, especially since she could feel his arousal pressing against her stomach.

"If you want this to happen," he said. "Be standing on my deck at seven p.m. tomorrow."

"But, what about the anticipation," she asked with a devilish grin.

"That was forty years ago, and a lot of water has passed under the bridge since then. Just be there."

"I've got to go," Henry said. "Now you know more about me than I ever thought you would be interested in learning." He got up to walk to the door and Yvonne reached to stop him.

She held him tightly, smiling as she said, "There is one more thing for certain I want to know," Then she kissed him and let him leave.

That kiss almost broke Henry's resolve. "Goodnight" he said, as he quickly walked out, noticing the nights were finally cooling from the intense summer heat. The walk to his car was exactly what he needed. He thought of her until he collapsed in his recliner, falling asleep.

Yvonne set her alarm before she crawled into bed. For the first time in years, she was excited about tomorrow.

Chapter 10

When her alarm clock went off, Yvonne was already awake and brushing her teeth. She returned to the nightstand beside her bed to turn it off. After rinsing her mouth, she went straight to the kitchen to get the coffee she had made before stepping out on the balcony. No one was there. It was still ten minutes or so till sunrise, but she knew he was on his way.

Henry woke up as usual, just before his alarm, noticing that he had slept in his clothes. He never did that but last night was an exception. Most mornings, he was filled with morbid thoughts and an impending sense of doom. Not this morning. Today, he felt like a boy on Christmas Day with one major exception: he knew the present, it was the unwrapping he longed to do. On the way to the place where he stood each morning, his thoughts were of Yvonne until the sun broke through the horizon. Then he spoke to Virginia aloud:

"I miss you, girlfriend. The past few months without you have been the worst of my entire life. Most days I think about going to the roof with my forty-five and joining you, ending all this sadness and grief. When I said you had to go before me it was only because I had no idea what it would be like without you. Bringing your ashes to this spot had such a feeling of finality. We were married longer than I was ever single and almost twice as long as you were single. I am grateful each day that it is me standing here and not you. For you to be in the depths of despair, grief beyond description, never to know the answer to why our time was cut short is a burden I gladly bear for you. I am not able to endure a life of loneliness and a wonderful woman has entered my life. If not for her there is a certainty that I would be joining, you in less than a year. You were the most jealous woman I ever knew so I know you would not want to know, but I must tell you. It has been thirty-two years since I had sex with a woman that wasn't you. I know it is not possible for you to give me your blessing and would not even if you could but when she shows up, if she shows up tonight, let there be something specific that only you and I know. I still and always will love you."

Yvonne watched him walk purposefully to the same spot each day. *How does he know exactly where to go?* She thought. *In the future, she would ask, but not today.* He stood there motionless until the sun was completely clear, then began to walk towards his house. Henry turned to look towards her balcony, seeing her there in the morning light. He was tempted to run to her house, but the decision was hers.

He waved. Yvonne saw him and thought as she waved back, *This was the first time he ever looked back towards me.* She knew he was thinking about her, only hoping it was as much as she was thinking about him. Her coffee was nearly gone and besides, she had some personal maintenance to take care of before tonight. While she was getting dressed for work, the thoughts of what to wear, how much to wear, makeup, no makeup, hair up, hair down, were flooding her mind. After work, she would stop by the nail and wax spa. The evening was filling her with such a sense of anticipation that she began to have doubts. These thoughts were romance-novel thoughts, the kind that never happened in real life, just the kind that sad neglected women read about. Her romance novel had turned into a tragic horror story. She had to just stop thinking, get dressed, and go to work because there was no way he could live up to these expectations. Then she remembered the kiss, his hand in her hair, on her butt, and that bulge against her stomach; Yvonne held out hope that he could.

Yvonne went to work just like she did every day. She went to her desk almost as mechanically as a clock. At eight o'clock, she turned her computer on, answered a phone call, signed a veteran in to see his mental health provider, and looked back at the clock. *Eight o' one.* "What the hell!" She almost yelled. *Just don't look at the clock,* Yvonne told herself. *It is agonizing how long a minute is when you are anticipating something exhilarating happening in the future.*

Henry decided to tidy up his house. A little mopping, dusting, straightening up the place, and of course pickle juice. Whenever his football teams were preparing for a game in the heat of August, they would always drink pickle juice before the game to prevent muscles from cramping. Under no circumstances would a cramp interrupt the activities he had planned for later. For lunch, he had tuna salad with whole wheat bread. He would not eat anything else for the rest of the day. Those stomach issues had always given him grief whenever he was anxious about performing on the field or in the coaching box. No food for five hours before the contest. Well, this was not a contest, but he did expect to give a performance. Then, he went to the bedroom, stripping the sheets off to wash and dry them. Even though they had never been slept on, he wanted them to be soft, aromatic, and perfect. All the pillows except two were put in Virginia's closet with her other things. Then, he closed her closet door; something he had never done before. As soon as he closed it, he reopened it. There was a shelf in the back of the closet where she kept scented candles. Mostly, he didn't like them, but there was one with a cinnamon chocolate aroma, which he thought would be nice for this evening. He also picked up four unscented candles as well.

Yvonne told her supervisor she had an appointment so she would need to get off work a couple of hours early. Her supervisor assumed it was a doctor's or dentist's appointment. She just didn't know the appointment was at a nail and spa salon. As she was walking out the door, an old vet from the Korean War was sitting near the door, waiting on his ride. He commented, "There's some pep in your step, young lady, got a hot date tonight?"

"I do indeed," she replied.

"Let me know if he mistreats you and I'll take care of him for you."

"Thanks, he won't," were her last words to him.

Soon she was at the salon. She had to choose how to get her nails and toes done. She decided on a classic French mani/pedi as well as wax. For the hour and a half, she was there. The conversations with the stylists kept her distracted, except for the wax stylist who told her about a cold compress after a warm bath would remove the bumps that inevitably rise after hair removal. She wanted to be as perfect as she could, with no bumps, uneven nails, or tough skin on her feet. When she got back in her car, Yvonne began to think about what she would do with her hair and what she would wear.

After lunch, Henry had his cleaning done so he drove back to Wilmington Island to get his hair cut, and to buy some flowers. All through his marriage, he had cut his hair. Now he kept it just a bit longer but could never taper it exactly the right way. When he returned home, he took one of the roses from the arrangement to place individual petals on the bed. He had ironed the sheets, and pillowcases, fluffed the pillows, and folded down the comforter. When he was finished, he stopped, looking at the room with the candles, the flowers, as well as the overall preparations he had made. A thought came to him, *Damn, I've turned into Suzie Homemaker.* He went to the kitchen to prepare a meal he hoped to eat much later that night. He had chicken breasts with a parmesan aioli. This would be for after so it would be okay, especially if they both ate the garlic, some steamed veggies, and a strawberry cheesecake.

When all his Betty Crocker and Suzie Homemaker business was done, he could finally focus on preparing himself. He went through one set of his normal weightlifting routine but did several sets of curls. Curls are for the girls, they always told their players. Sometimes when he had been feeling particularly motivated, he would flex his biceps to show the young guys what was possible. Those thoughts didn't last long though. Those days were all in the past, his only competition now was old age, a battle he knew he would inevitably lose but would fight anyway. Stop thinking like that, he told himself. Tonight he would not be or act fifty-seven, no. Tonight, he would be forty. That age suited him fine, not too young to be frivolous but, not too old to be out of the action. He showered, shaved, and began to get dressed. He knew it was still forty-five minutes until she was due to be there. *Please be here*, he thought, so he went to a section of his closet where the clothes that he never wore were hung. On his thirtieth anniversary, his wife bought him an athletic cut tuxedo. No frills, just a nice black tuxedo with a bow tie. He hated bow ties with two exceptions, his tuxedo, and his dress blues. Henry didn't care what Yvonne wore; he didn't intend for her to be wearing it for very long.

It was a quarter to seven when Henry stepped out of the bedroom, lit the candles, and waited for Yvonne. As he did, an apparition was standing in front of the door on his deck. It was Virginia. As he walked towards the door, he realized it was not Virginia, but her hair and dress sure gave him that impression.

Yvonne had decided to wear a white sheath dress that had a short zipper at the bottom of the open back and a clasp on the back of the neck. She had worn it once for Nate and the clasp had given him fits. Her hair had been pulled up and fastened so that her neck and face were completely exposed. On either side of her cheeks were spiral curls that hung down in front of her ears. She had decided on a minimum of makeup but, hoped he liked red lipstick. If she had looked in the drawer of his wife's vanity, it would have been the only color she saw.

He opened the door. "You are simply gorgeous, and early," he said, taking her hand as she entered.

And you remind me of James Bond, she thought but did not say. Instead, she said, "We look like we belong on a cake."

He admitted that they did, except this was better. "The man and woman on the cake never kiss," he said, bending down to kiss her. As he began to kiss her, he reached down and scooped her in his arms. "Um," she said, surprised at how quickly he had swept her off her feet. Then she welcomed his embrace, placing her head against his chest as he carried her towards the bedroom. He opened the door to reveal the preparations he had made. The room was completely dark except for the light coming from the candles. When she had been there before, she had not noticed the windows and balcony doors had blackout curtains.

He took her to the edge of the bed, sat her down, and said, "Wait here a moment."

There were candle stands in the corners of the room, as well as a scented candle on the center of a dresser. He walked over, extinguishing the scented candle. Its job was over, and a nice aroma of cinnamon and chocolate was hanging in the air. When he came back to her, he knelt to remove her shoes. Once her shoes were off, he helped her back to her feet.

"The room is beautiful," she said.

"Not compared to you," he said as their lips joined. *Christmas Day had arrived*, he thought. Virginia had a dress like this one. You needed both hands to undo the button from the cord which it fastened to, and after that, it was quickly released. Her dress was held up by his body being pressed against hers while his hands made their way to the zipper. All that was left now was to remove the wrapping.

Henry held her dress by the collar with one hand slowly allowing gravity to do its job until her breasts were exposed. *They were perfect,* he thought, *not pumped up with silicone or saline filler but beautifully formed by her genetics.* The gentle touch of the dress moving across them on its way to the floor had caused her nipples to harden. Then, he took the dress in both hands at her waist. Slowly lowering it until she could step out, he did not drop it on the floor but draped it over a chair. When he turned around, he could appreciate all she had done. There was still more unwrapping to do but not while she was standing. He turned back and swept her up again. This time, he placed his knee on the bed, gently laying her on the sheets and pillow. On his side of the bed was a valet which was soon covered with his clothing. He picked up a towel and placed it on his pillow before he got on the bed.

Yvonne could tell he was not completely aroused, but the thought of the girl in the Volkswagen suddenly crossed her mind as he made his way towards her, and she giggled.

"Not exactly the response I was hoping for," he said.

"Sorry, I don't know why, but I just thought about your

misadventure in the Volkswagen."

"Not tonight," he said. "And thank you."

"Thank you for what?" She said.

"The garter set is perfect, as well as my favorite, and for being here."

"Why did you get a towel?" She asked.

Henry said nothing. His smile said everything.

As he positioned himself at her side, they began to kiss. Now she could let herself go and soon, she had placed her leg over his. Henry's response was to reach down and, one by one, release the garter straps. Each one of the four straps was undone without her having to move her leg from its position on his. She was only beginning to appreciate his dexterity.

When he pushed her leg gently off his and created space between them, she was on her stomach before she had time to form a question. *No more thinking, just pleasure,* she thought. *This man can do whatever he wants.* Henry wanted to kiss every part of her body, so he slowly removed her stockings and started with her ankles. Slowly, he kissed his way up her body, taking his time so that no part would feel neglected or unappreciated. As he reached her neck, the kisses were accompanied by little nips from his teeth. He only bit hard enough for a reaction from her, the only marks he would leave would be in her memory.

As he repositioned himself at her side, she felt a much firmer grip on the back of her knee. He lifted her leg to place his leg between hers and pulled her leg up to his waist. The pressure of his leg against her began what she could only describe as a series of small seismic shocks. Henry was a geography teacher, and this could be described as a seismic storm, albeit orgasmic, but a storm, nonetheless. Each one increased in intensity with every touch.

As their kisses became more passionate, it was her turn to kiss him. Henry had bitten down on her tongue with just enough pressure to hold it, then he closed his lips around her tongue and held her tongue in his mouth. Yvonne had tried to control her responses to him, but this was something she had never experienced, and the sound Henry heard was one of pleasure. When he returned his tongue to her mouth, Yvonne was happy to reciprocate. As she was biting his tongue, his hand, which had been caressing her thigh, moved to the outside of her panties. He soon began to massage her in a way that he knew would gently elevate her pleasure. She let go of his tongue, her mouth still open, but her facial muscles tightened as she released a long sigh when he began to move his fingers.

The shocks were no longer small, the frequency was diminishing, but their intensity increased. Every muscle and nerve ending was now alive and pleading for more.

When she had broken the touch of their lips, Henry had just moved his attention to her neck. A mix of kisses and bites was exploring every part of her skin. He knew exactly where his wife got the most pleasure. Now, he would see if Yvonne reacted the same way. His teeth were in position, and as he bit, much harder than he had before, on the place where her neck and shoulder joined, the sound that came from Henry was the reflexive sound a person makes when they taste something incredibly savory, and Yvonne moaned louder.

He could tell she was becoming incredibly aroused, so he stopped kissing her neck and rolling her onto her back. *Why is he stopping,* she thought, but when he reached for the towel, she knew it would only get better. He unfolded the towel until it was folded in half and positioned it under her butt. Then he opened her legs and got between them. She reached around to pull him closer, but he kept his weight supported on his elbows as he lowered his lips to hers. The kiss was short but filled with passion. He began to move down her body, kissing the front as he had the back. When he got to her nipples, he gently took them in his teeth, tugging on them until they were completely erect.

Slowly, he kissed his way down her stomach.

The storm was now a fully-fledged earthquake, increasing in magnitude, and he was not even touching her yet. Her last rational thought was *that this was the best sex she ever had, and if he finished now, it would still be incredible.* That thought ended when he took her panties in his hands, ripping them at the crotch. Now, his kisses were everywhere except the one place she wanted him the most. His tongue caressed both of her thighs, making its way around the path the stylist had waxed for him. She could feel his breath, his arms wrapped around her legs, his fingers gently pulling her open. Her feet were now on his back, trying to pull him where she wanted him to go.

Henry could hear her moaning with every exhaled breath, so when his tongue finally touched her, it was a single loud groan.

She wanted him to break the Richter scale, but his tongue moved slowly, avoiding the place she wanted him to go. In vain, she began to move her hips back and forth to encourage him to speed up, but this was happening at his pace.

Now, her moans had been replaced by the same word over and over. "Oh! Oh! Oh! Oh! Oh! Don't stop," she pleaded in an anguished whisper.

As she looked down, she could see he was wiping her off his lips and beard. He positioned himself above her with his weight on his knees and one hand while the other positioned himself.

"Yes," was the word she whispered.

As he began, he moved slowly, each movement taking him further. The earthquakes continued one after the other, but now she could feel the pressure building from down within her. Slowly rising, slowly increasing with each thrust of his hips. She could no longer kiss him, not because of her smell on his lips, but because she did not have the focus to kiss back. He continued to kiss and bite her neck, moving from one side to the other.

After what seemed like an eternity to her, he pushed himself fully inside of her, and the frequency and intensity of his thrusts increased one after the other. The pressure was rising like lava in a magma chamber; the eruption would soon happen, and she wanted him to go faster. Instead, he stopped.

The anguish that he was finished was not even a complete thought when he made his way back down. This time, his tongue had a singular focus, a single spot, but gently moved from one side to the other and up and down in small circular movements.

When she didn't think the pleasure could become any more intense, he slid a finger inside her, gently massaging her like he knew what he was doing. *Oh my god,* she thought, *he does.* Any thoughts of any expectations she had before vaporized as the pleasure she was experiencing removed the ability she normally possessed for rational thought.

As his tongue maintained a steady rhythm, she could feel the quake beginning, and this was going to be off the Richter scale.

Suddenly, all the smaller quakes joined together, creating a cataclysmic event that shook her to her bones. She was not aware of what she was saying, but it was. "Oh My God," over and over, increasing in frequency and volume until a final "Oh My GOOOOOOOOOOOOOOOD!" Her thighs tightened on his head; her pelvis lifted from the towel, pressing into his face. Then she grabbed him by the head pulling his face towards hers.

Whatever manners, decency, or social conformity she had previously known was now gone. At this moment, there was only one thing in the world that mattered to her, and that was him.

This time he placed his chest against hers, his hands could not support his weight since they had a firm grip on each cheek of her soft curvy ass. As he began to push himself inside her, she began to bite his shoulder while her fingernails dug into his back. Her words were spoken in a much deeper tone than she normally spoke, were a command more than a request.

"Hard and fast," she demanded.

Now it was his turn, Henry began to increase the speed and force of each thrust.

For Yvonne, the earthquake and volcanic eruption had joined forces. *This must have been what it was like when the Earth was being formed.* This was not a thought she was consciously having because she was distracted by how much harder he got as he was about to finish.

Henry moved his hands beside Yvonne's shoulders so he could arch his own back, finishing as deep inside of her as he could. She was grabbing his hips, holding him in that position until he collapsed on top of her, burying his face into her neck and gently kissing her until he was completely empty.

When their pounding heart rates finally calmed, Henry raised and used the towel to wipe Yvonne and himself before throwing it on the floor.

"This is what the towel is for," he finally answered with a very satisfied smile.

When he lay down, he was on his back, spread out like an eagle. Yvonne put one arm under her pillow, draping the other arm and leg across him with her face against his chest. Then, the thought occurred to her. *This is the position his wife was in for every photo in that room.*

She closed her eyes for a moment, enjoying the satisfaction of knowing what had just happened to her had never been written in any novel. This was real, and this belonged to her. That was her last thought before she drifted off into complete contentment.

Henry was already there.

Chapter 11

Henry was looking at her face when she eventually opened her eyes, "Hello, beautiful," he said.

Yvonne smiled and replied, "Hello, handsome."

Their nap was just a good excuse for catching their breath, only lasting about ten minutes. Henry rolled over, sitting on the edge of the bed for just a moment before rising to go to the bathroom.

"Sorry!" Yvonne said in a tone of complete insincerity.

"For what?" Was Henry's reply.

"Look at your back," she said with a smile that indicated her satisfaction.

When he did look, the signs of Yvonne's pleasure carved by her fingernails covered his back, and some were slightly bleeding. His father had always told him you can't feel pain in two places at once; perhaps he was right, and perhaps he wasn't, but this Henry knew to be true. Whatever pain Yvonne had inflicted didn't surpass the pleasure she provided.

"I've had worse," was all he said.

She heard the shower and decided to join him. Sometime during their adventure, her hair had fallen, and as she began to stand, the rest of her almost fell. Her legs were almost useless, weak to the point of quivering if she stood the wrong way or had too much of her weight on just one leg. She attempted to put her hair back up as she walked into the bathroom, taking tiny steps.

"Leave it down," he said. "I love your hair down."

Yvonne paused. *Did he just say he loved her? Or was it just an expression? Did the words hair down negate the, I love you?* With these thoughts flying through her brain, she stepped into the shower. *Was that sponge in there the last time she was here? And she was sure the bath soap was not.* While she was thinking, Henry had lathered up the sponge but pulled her to him.

His shower had a rain head as well as a regular head, so they both stood with the water washing over them. Henry began to wash every part of her body. His touch was soft and respectful, like the way people touch priceless artifacts. When he asked her to lift her leg so he could wash her foot, she felt her other leg begin to tremble. Quickly, he steadied her, guiding her to the seat.

"Are you OK?" He asked.

"I need to start working out to keep up with you," she smiled. "I've never had this reaction to sex before."

"Is that good or bad?" He asked while washing each toe individually.

"Oh," she said with a long exhale. "It was good." *Mind-blowing, nerve-crashing, orgasmic euphoria,* she thought but did not say. Her mind tried to think of a time when sex with Nate had been like this. There had been earthquakes and volcanos for sure, but she had always been able to walk afterward. Perhaps it was just so long, but perhaps Nate was a musician in bed, and Henry was a composer.

While she was letting all these thoughts run through her mind, Henry simply stepped back and washed himself with what could only be described as swift efficiency. Then he turned the water off, grabbed a towel, and began to dry her with the same meticulous scrutiny he had washed her with, almost surgical.

"Perfect," he said.

"What's perfect?"

"Your skin, he said, there are no birthmarks, freckles, or scars." He stated.

"The scars are all on the inside," Yvonne said.

"And those are the worst," he replied, handing her the towel and asking if she would dry his back?

"Why were you examining me?" She was genuinely curious as to his answer.

"Well," he started. "When you are not around, and I close my eyes, the image of you in my mind must be exact in every detail," he replied.

Henry had placed two choices of clothing for her to wear on the vanity: a long cotton nightshirt or a set of pajamas as well as a pair of black lace panties.

"Did these belong to your wife?" She asked.

"Yes, but those were things she never wore or didn't like, but she wouldn't throw away."

"Why did you include these she said, holding the panties?"

"My wife always wore panties; she said she felt naked without them."

"I don't mind naked," Yvonne replied, pulling the nightshirt over her head.

"Me neither," Henry said as he put on a black pair of pajama pants and a red T-shirt two sizes too big, which had a big letter G on the front.

"So, do you spend time thinking about me?" She asked.

"Yes, the part of my day I spend thinking about anything else is getting very little. I thought the vacuum created when my wife died would eventually consume me, but then you had breakfast with me. By the way, I smell supper. Are you hungry?"

"Starving" was Yvonne's answer. "What smells so good?"

Henry looked back at Yvonne with a devilish smile and said, "You."

This was not different from any other meal they had or would share. Henry again cleared the table before she thought about what she was missing, "You want some coffee and cheesecake?" He asked.

"Just a small piece of cheesecake," she replied, so he cut the piece in half. When he brought her saucer and fork, she saw what he had done and thought. *This must have been what they were like together.*

When a couple of bites of cheesecake were gone, she reached for his plate, saying, "I'll take that for you."

Henry watched every step as she walked into the kitchen and turned on the water. As if on command, he stood up, walked up behind her, and slightly pressed her against the sink with his body, but, this time, his hands went directly to her breasts as he kissed her neck.

I've never enjoyed washing dishes so much in my life, she thought. There she was in a nightshirt with a towel wrapped around her head, and Henry followed her to the kitchen, showing his appreciation while making her feel desirable all at the same time.

Suddenly, she realized something.

"What is your name?" Yvonne asked.

"Henry," was his reply, just briefly thinking she might have lost brain cells with her orgasm.

"No, your entire name, I have no idea what your full name is." She explained.

"My name is William Henry Morgan, and yours?"

Such a strong name, she thought, *for a strong man.* "Yvonne Nichole Bennett," she replied.

"Is that the married name or your maiden name?" He asked.

"My maiden name was Brown."

"Well, Mrs. Yvonne Nichole Brown-Bennett, I am pleased to have made your acquaintance."

"And I, yours, Mr. William Henry Morgan."

She held out her right hand for him as if on cue, he bent at the waist to kiss her hand. As his lips reached her fingers, she crossed her legs, acknowledging his bow with a curtsey.

As his kiss ended, she said, "There is no hyphenated name. I stopped being Miss Brown when I became Mrs. Bennett."

As he stood up, he smiled and said, "I stand corrected, Mrs. Bennett. Would you accompany me to the roof?"

Briefly, he stopped by his buffet to pour them both a glass of wine.

They were both smiling as they walked to the stairs. She had not been on the roof before, so this would, without a doubt, provide an incredible view.

As they emerged onto the roof, it was more spectacular than she could have imagined. The moon was waning and would not rise until early in the morning. The sky was clear, the breeze light and the tide was coming in, so the crash of the waves was loud, blocking out all other noises, and his house had a view of the stars which was incredible.

"It's beautiful up here," she said.

"It is now," he said, taking her hand while walking over to the loungers. She sat down, and he moved the table from between the chairs so he could be positioned directly beside hers.

There was no conversation for a while. Each occasionally took sips of the wine and relaxed in the afterglow of the evening. Two people gazing into the universe, each letting their minds guide their thoughts. Not only were they connected by their hands, but their minds were also moving in the same direction.

The sky suddenly lit up with the flash of lightning off to the southwest. A storm was approaching, but it was not due to arrive till just before dawn. That flash was soon followed by another, but there was no thunder; the storm was too distant, and the waves were too loud.

"Do you have to work tomorrow?" Henry asked as he broke the silence.

"I am supposed to be in at eight," she replied.

"It is going to be raining in the morning, and you will get soaked getting to your car. Not that I mind you being wet at all, he said, but would you consider taking a sick day and staying here with me tonight?"

"I have never taken a sick day or any day off from work in ten years," she said, "I'll have to call first thing in the morning."

"That won't be a problem," Henry smiled, "I am an early riser."

"I don't have a toothbrush," Yvonne stated.

"In the other bathroom, I have an unopened pack so you can pick your color and toothpaste, makeup remover, cotton balls, Q-Tips, and anything else you think you might need. If I don't have it, I'll get it." He said, attempting to prevent any further statements that could indicate second thoughts.

"Okay, okay, I get it," Yvonne said, smiling. "I'm not going... before she could complete her sentence," she yawned, "...anywhere."

Henry stood up and offered her his hand. As she took it, he pulled her up from the chair. He placed her hand on his arm with his hand on hers as they walked toward the stairs; she placed her other hand on his and her head against his shoulder. He would get the wine glasses later.

When they got downstairs, he entered the other guest bedroom, emerging with a small container of sundries for anything she might need.

After he finished brushing his teeth, he thought, *if Yvonne is going to be here, I need to move my things back into the other bathroom.* As he entered the bedroom, Yvonne was already in bed. However, there was a nervousness on her face that had not been there before. She could tell he saw something was wrong as he went to the other side of the bed and removed his pajamas, she asked, "Will you do something for me?"

"There is nothing in heaven or on earth I wouldn't do for you," he vowed.

She turned to her side and faced him; he could see she was not wearing the nightgown, but the look on her face bothered him.

"You will be the only man I have ever slept with other than my father, which doesn't count and Nate. We always did something well said, and did something she corrected herself before we went to sleep. You don't have to mean the words, but would you say them for me..."

Henry pressed his finger against her lips before she could finish.

"Goodnight," he said, staring into her eyes.

"Goodnight," she said, finishing with a kiss.

"Sweet dreams,"

"Sweet dreams," she replied again, punctuated with a kiss.

"I love you, Yvonne."

Her reply was sincere as tears filled her eyes; "I love you too, Henry."

He kissed her again.

"Something like that?" He said.

"Exactly that," was her reply, "How did you know?"

"My wife and I said the same things for thirty-three years. Thank you for that."

Thank you for everything you did today: the candles, the flowers, and all your preparation. It was like a honeymoon.

It was all worth it as soon as you stood at my door. This bed we made love on today was the first time anyone had ever been on it; my wife and I never slept on it or anything else.

Yvonne then put her arm and leg over him as she had earlier that evening. She leaned towards him for one last kiss before nestling her head against his chest.

Henry was thinking how familiar this evening had been. *From the dress to the passion and the goodnight kisses. He had loved his wife for thirty-three years and loved her still, but he knew in his heart he also loved Yvonne.*

Whether he meant it or not, Yvonne thought, *she had heard Henry say he loved her.* It was so comforting to not be in bed alone and to experience those goodnight kisses again. She had always believed sex with another man would only cause feelings of guilt and infidelity; it did not. Nate was gone; besides, he had told her to move on and find love. She just could never imagine loving another man. A week ago, she had never met this man. Now she was in his bed and happily so. Tomorrow, she would call in to work. For the first time in ten years, she had something better to do. She didn't want to go back to her house either. The only thing she wanted to do was stay where she was, tonight, tomorrow, and forever. *Whoever else this man was or whatever else he had done,* Yvonne knew she loved him.

Henry turned over on his side, facing away from Yvonne. This had been how he had always fallen asleep in the past, and sleep was rapidly approaching. She did not let him go but simply kept her arm and leg in contact until he was settled. Now, she was snuggling up to him the way Nate always did to her. She was unaware of when she drifted off to sleep or turned over on her other side. The next thing Yvonne was aware of was a sudden loud crash of thunder, which woke her from her sleep. Instead of being afraid, as she normally would have been, the feeling of Henry against her body reassured her, allowing her to return to her dreams quickly.

Chapter 12

At five-thirty, Henry woke up as he did every day. However, today was different from every other day because Yvonne was beside him. He turned over towards her, enjoying the early moments of waking to embrace this beautiful young woman who had assaulted him on the beach. There was a thunderstorm raging much as his passion had been. No sunrise this morning, instead, he would simply hold Yvonne until she woke from her sleep.

He held her just like that for an hour. When she opened her eyes, he could tell she was still mostly asleep as he told her, "Good morning, beautiful."

"Morning," was all she could muster. Something had died in her mouth, and she had to pee.

As she staggered towards the toilet, he was about to burst from nature's call, so he went to the guest room to relieve himself and brush his teeth. When he returned, Yvonne was still in the bathroom, so he climbed back into bed. He could hear her moving around but wondered what she could be doing.

When Yvonne emerged from the bathroom, her hair was brushed and in a ponytail. Her legs had regained their strength, so she wanted to return the favor for the way Henry made her feel, and the only thing she had as she climbed into bed was a towel.

After Yvonne pulled the towel, she threw the covers off the bed. She made sure the towel was folded in half, placing it on the bed beside Henry. Then she covered him with her body, lowering her lips to his.

Henry's hands caressed every part of Yvonne that he could reach, enjoying the softness and warmth of her skin until his hands reached her back. From there, his hands found the curve of her ass, and his touch became firmer as he began to grab as much of her in each hand as he could.

Yvonne pulled her lips away from his. She smiled as she started to kiss his chest, slowly moving past his navel until she was able to kiss him another way.

The storm had been powerful with thunder, lightning, and heavy rain. While the storm outside was subsiding, a storm of another type was building, and Yvonne was encouraging it with every touch of her tongue. It did not take long for her to have him ready for the next wave, which was approaching. Yvonne positioned herself straddling him and began to make love to him.

Henry thought how incredibly beautiful this woman was. He also tried to remember the last time he had morning sex. Neither he nor his wife had been particularly amorous in the morning, at least not until after coffee and breakfast. *The last time was years ago, and damn,* he thought. *I am old, and Yvonne, this beautiful woman riding him, was probably in high school.* He forced himself to think about many things to interrupt the sensations from Yvonne.

Yvonne was not aware of the sounds she was making as her hips moved faster, but with every back-and-forth motion, as she exhaled, there was an audible pant.

When the panting stopped, every muscle in her face had tightened, her motions became circular, and she let out a loud sigh. While she was enjoying the lava flow from the volcano, Henry placed his hands under her thighs and pulled her hips to his chest.

Thinking about washing his car had allowed him to control himself. He could now return these thoughts and actions to her. This time, he took his tongue directly to the source of her earthquakes. Yvonne was in control of this now, and she moved her hips to change the placement of his tongue. No seismic storms this time, just a rapid build to a catastrophic quake. When her legs tightened against his head, he rolled her over onto the towel.

Good thing she brought it, too. As quickly as he could, he wiped his face while getting his body in position. He grabbed a pillow and pushed it under Yvonne's back, then he positioned himself. He wanted to be sure to give her a proper thanks for her efforts this morning, so he placed the back of her knees against his biceps, lifting her knees to her shoulders.

This was not like yesterday. As he entered, he pushed himself in at once. Yvonne moaned loudly.

The noises Yvonne was making were keeping pace with Henry's hips. He had stopped thinking about his car, the weather, or anything other than this woman, and the feeling he could tell was building inside him. He was raising and dropping his hips slowly at first, but now he was increasing until it was as fast and hard as he was able. Normally, Henry only made noise if he was kissing her neck, but not this time. As he exploded, an involuntary groan of relief, which lasted the duration of his orgasm, landed on Yvonne's ears. He held himself inside her as forcefully as he could until his orgasm completely subsided. Then he released her left leg first and her right, supporting most of his weight on his elbows but keeping as much contact with her body as he could as he rested his head on her shoulder.

Yvonne's breathing had slowed as well; now, each breath was deep with a long exhalation. As Henry started to rise, she grabbed him and said, "Not yet, aftershocks."

When her hands relaxed on his hips, he withdrew and wiped them both with the towel and lay beside her. It was several minutes before either one of them moved.

"Stay here," he said to Yvonne as he got out of bed.

"Um, hum," she replied without opening her mouth. Yvonne was certain that if her legs quivered yesterday, they would be completely done today. Her eyes were closed, and her breathing had slowed as she allowed her brain to reset her body. She was not aware of anything around her or the fifteen minutes that passed.

When she opened her eyes, Henry had lifted her off the bed, *carrying her to the bathroom like a princess,* she thought. "I have to pee," she said. So, he sat her on the toilet. She had her elbows on her knees and her face in her hand when she said the first thing that popped into her head. "Did you ever notice how difficult it is to pee after sex?" she asked as she looked up, smiling at him.

"I still can't go," he replied as her water began to flow.

When she was done, he picked her up and took her over to the tub. He dipped her foot in the water and asked if it was too hot.

"No," she answered. *When did he fill the tub?* She thought to herself.

He lowered her into the tub and walked out of the bathroom.

Glorious, she thought, *this tub is simply glorious.* She remembered her first look at this tub, wanting to relax in it, but never imagined it would be like this.

When Henry returned, he had two cups of coffee. His was black; hers had three level teaspoons of sugar and four teaspoons of milk.

She took a sip of the coffee, amazed it was exactly how she liked it, even better than she made for herself. Then she remembered him saying anything was better if someone made it for you.

"How did you know the way I liked my coffee?" She asked.

"I watched you make it before." He replied, surprised by the question.

The tub, the sex, the coffee, or the total of everything that had happened caused her to not think about what she was saying or even care. This man had made her feel like she never thought she would ever feel again.

She looked at him and said, "I love you."

Without even a moment of pause, Henry replied, "And I'll love you for the rest of my life, so when the rain stops, let's go to your house and get the things you need to stay here."

"Hope you're hungry," he said. "I'm making waffles."

"Give me about twenty more minutes in this tub," she said. Laying her head back and relaxing.

"Take your time," he said as he walked out of the bathroom.

He heard the hot water run twice before she emerged from the bathroom. When she did, she wore the pajama set on the vanity. She had also blow-dried her hair and applied lotion.

Henry walked out of the kitchen to meet her. He put his arms around her, lifting her off the floor so she didn't have to tilt her head for his kiss. As she kissed him, she remembered how her daddy used to pick her up like this and dance with her when she was a little girl. The feeling of love and security that filled her made her think, why would she ever leave?

"Yes," she said.

"Yes, to what?" Henry asked.

"Yes, I'll move in."

"I already knew that," he replied. "When you didn't immediately say no."

"I have one condition," Yvonne said in a tone that he knew was non-negotiable.

"Anything," was his immediate reply.

"You don't know what it is," she said, puzzled.

"It doesn't matter," he stated. "If I have to kill someone, I have a friend or two that will help me hide the body."

At first, she thought he was serious, but his smile at the end let her know he was joking.

"It's not that serious," she stated. "You just have to marry me."

Henry's expression became more serious as he looked at her, slowly lowering her to the floor.

"Don't move," he said.

He went back into the bedroom; he was only in there seconds before returning, on one knee in front of her and reaching for her left hand, then asked, "Yvonne Nichole Bennett, will you be my wife?" As he asked her, he placed a wide band with a circular cluster of diamonds on her finger.

"You know I will," she said, as she pulled him up for a kiss.

"Did this belong to your wife?" Yvonne asked.

"It always will," he replied.

Yvonne had taken her wedding ring off the day she found out Nate had died. There was an anger festering for years because he left her. Suddenly, all that anger was gone, and the only thing she remembered about Nate was his love for her and the fact he had the foresight to let her know that if this day came, he wanted her to be happy and loved.

"Will you be upset if sometimes I wear the ring Nate bought for me?" She asked.

Henry had never seen a ring on Yvonne's finger, and there was no impression that one had been removed. "Yvonne, you may wear anything that makes you comfortable or nothing at all. I prefer nothing at all."

As Henry took the last bite of his waffle, she quickly gathered up the dishes, moving to the sink. Soon, he was pressed right up against her with his hands cupping and enjoying her breasts. His kisses began at the base of her neck, slowly moving up to her ear. After his tongue made its way from her ear lobe back around to where it began, he whispered, "I love you."

She replied in kind, thinking that she would never let him stand here again. Looking outside, she could see the rain had stopped.

Chapter 13

When Yvonne ended her call, she came back inside.

"Did you take tomorrow off?" Henry asked.

"No, I took the rest of my life off if that's okay with you, and can I borrow your truck?"

"I'm overjoyed, but don't you want me to come help you?"

"There are things I must do by myself," she said. "Things I must resolve. A ghost I must make peace with."

Henry understood, more than she knew. No, he stopped himself from thinking that; she knew exactly. And instead of saying anything, he simply walked to his key rack, bringing her the keys and a long embrace followed by a kiss.

Yvonne picked up her phone as she walked to the elevator. Turning, she blew him a kiss before descending. "Back in a while," she said before she closed the door.

Any joy, happiness, or purpose left him when Yvonne closed the elevator door. A melancholy feeling suddenly overcame him along with those feelings of impending doom and grief. He was a cheater and a liar; this he knew in his heart. Now he was going to have to break his vow to his wife again. Either he was going to love, honor, and cherish Yvonne for the rest of their lives, or he was going to have to make her wait until his morning vow was over. He did not want to make her wait. He did not want to wait. He was now angry at his wife for the first time in years. He had asked her for something specific, something only he and she knew, and nothing had come. The good night ritual did not count. How could it? Yvonne and Nate had done the same thing, as far as he knew, hundreds, maybe thousands of couples did. There was no way he could forgive himself without some recognition that Virginia had forgiven him. His rationale had completely left him; he wanted forgiveness from a dead person for something she did not know occurred. There was no logic or reasoning behind his feelings; they were just that, feelings. So much he wished she had not died.

"Why did you leave me?" he screamed, as his tears began to flow. "I wasn't ready for goodbye."

"It should be you here with me, not her."

"I didn't appreciate you enough to be faithful, and I don't deserve her."

"I'm so sorry I cheated on you," he cried. "Please forgive me. PLEASE!" he screamed.

Yvonne did not hear him yell. By the time Henry started screaming, she was in the truck with the engine running and the garage door opening. Just sitting there holding the steering wheel took her back to being sixteen again. Nate would let her drive his truck whenever she asked; in fact, this is the first vehicle she learned to drive. So many firsts occurred in this truck. She let her mind go back this time to recall all those firsts, including the last time she saw him in his truck. This time, for the first time, her memories did not bring back the pain or grief. Nate had told her to sell this truck, buy her something frivolous, and find new love. If ghosts can alter events in our lives, she was sure Nate intervened so Henry would buy this truck and become her new love. She had met Henry the day she lost Nate's letter. A letter he had asked her to burn. For Yvonne, any doubts about Henry or their life together were settled. She rushed up the steps to her condo. This would not take long at all. Only a few items of clothing, some bath items, and a photo album. There were pictures she wanted to share with Henry. The main thing was her wedding ring. It was in a drawer on the nightstand beside her bed along with two other rings; she had never been a jewelry person anyway. She liked clothes. Nate's ring she immediately put on her right ring finger, and for a moment held up her hands to look at them both. Soon, Yvonne put all her jewelry on, grabbed her things, and locked the house. As she was leaving, she noticed an envelope was on the floor right in front of her door. Somehow, she had missed it when she came into the condo. There was a note on the envelope which said the neighbor below her, an elderly woman named Helen, had found it on her balcony days ago. When she opened the envelope, it was Nate's letter. She pulled the truck into the garage rather than back it in like Henry always did. She was in a hurry to get back inside and put her few things away. When she opened the door to the elevator, she saw Henry sitting on the deck. She put his keys and her jewelry on the counter, but she kept on both wedding sets as she joined him on the deck. She also had the envelope.

As she got closer, she could see he was holding the white outfit he wore each day.

"What is the matter?" She asked, bending over to kiss his cheek.

"I'm a lying, cheating, deceitful bastard," he said.

"Not to me," said Yvonne. "Or did something happen in the thirty minutes I was gone?"

He looked up to see her smiling, and immediately those feelings passed. He explained how his moods turned melancholy whenever she wasn't near him, and it was stupid for him to feel that way.

She sat on his lap, and when he finished, she told him it was not stupid for him to feel that way. "My neighbor Helen put this under my door. I would like you to read it." Henry took the envelope from her hand and opened the letter.

"The love of my life," it began. Henry read it slowly, trying to imagine the difficulty Nate had in writing it, knowing this was the third version of this letter. He had never written anything like this for Virginia. As he got to the end, it was the "My Wife, My Lover, My Friend" that sent tears down his face. Henry thought about the anguish he must have gone through to write a letter like this and how much he must have loved her to the point he was willing to have her find love again. With another man. With him.

Then Yvonne showed him the ring Nate had bought for her.

"I see why you would want to wear it," he said. "That is quite a rock."

Yvonne told him she had not worn it since the day the chaplain arrived out of anger.

She really does understand everything, Henry thought.

"I want to show you photos if you don't mind," Yvonne implored.

He was walking beside her as she went to the counter where she had sat everything except the suitcase with her clothes when Henry stopped. She looked back and saw him staring at something on the counter. And as she turned to look, she said, "What?"

"That ring, the one that has a swirly top," he said, pointing.

"This silver one," she said, holding it in her hand.

"I've never seen you wear it before," he said.

"You nor anyone else has ever seen me wear a ring until today. I'm not much of a ring person," she explained, "besides, it's a little big for any finger but my bird finger," she said, smiling as she demonstrated.

"Where did you get it?" His voice had a nervousness she had not heard or even believed he could make.

She took it off her finger and handed it to him. "I found it," she said with a questioning expression.

Before she could say anything further, he interrupted, while looking at the ring, "On the sink of the women's bathroom at the Walmart on Wilmington Island?"

"Yes," she said, "How could you know that?"

"Let's go sit down on the sofa and I will tell you," he said.

Chapter 14

"It was the summer of nineteen ninety, my wife was huge, and she was almost full term with my daughter. We had just moved from Ft. Benning to Ft. Stewart into our first house. It was hard for her to unpack and get us settled in while lugging her belly around but, after the first week, she pretty much had everything settled. Not that we had that much stuff anyway."

As he was talking, Yvonne could hear a calmness beginning in his voice and see a change in the expression on his face. She was not sure if it was the story or something else.

"My son was only fifteen months old and staying with his granny—excuse me, my wife's mother—for the weekend. This would be the last weekend we would share together before the war."

Yvonne looked a bit confused, "What war?" she asked.

"Operation Desert Storm," he said, knowing that is how most people referred to it. "The first Gulf War."

"Nothing was ever the same after that," he said, as his voice trailed off.

She could tell these were old memories and while the scars had healed, the wounds could feel fresh if prodded correctly.

"Anyway," he continued, "she wanted to go to River Street. There is a fantastic candy shop there, and she was craving pralines. After she had her pralines, we were walking and passed a store, a jewelry shop called Cassandra's. The owner made hand-crafted jewelry…"

"Oh, my God!" Yvonne screamed as she burst into tears. "Is this that ring?"

As Henry said "Yes," a tear streamed down his cheek.

"We must have spent thirty minutes looking at everything before she saw this," he said, holding the ring. "I told her it looked ridiculous, but she loved the unique look of it."

"The owner explained to us he had difficulty crafting it and it was too big for most women's fingers, so he would cut us a deal. She was thrilled that no other woman would have a ring like it, so I think I paid maybe twenty-five bucks for it."

He held the ring up and closed his hand around it. "The best twenty-five bucks I will ever spend," he said.

"She would wear this ring everywhere. It had fit her right ring finger until after our daughter was born, then she wore it on her right bird finger too. Often, she would show me the ring holding up the finger it was on, and say, how does it look? Exactly the way you did."

"It was February of twenty-fifteen when my daughter was getting married and she had told her mother she wanted to borrow something old to kill two birds, as it were, with one stone. If it had been blue, she could have got three birds I guess," he said, laughing.

"Something old, something new, something borrowed, something blue," Yvonne chimed in.

"Exactly," said Henry.

"The only caveat my wife told her was not to lose it. It was her favorite ring."

"Before the wedding even took place, my daughter and wife went to the store to get who knows what. My daughter had to use the restroom, so she took the ring off to wash her hands. Her phone rang and as she was trying to dry her hands while answering the phone, she turned away from the sink. When she got to the parking lot after they finished shopping, she realized it was gone."

"My wife told me she came back to the car crying that she had lost the ring."

"Over the years we would check pawn shops, craft jewelers, and even Cassandra's every time we were on River Street. There was always a look of remorse on her face when it could not be replaced."

"I don't know why I kept it instead of taking it to customer service," she said.

"If you had, then one of them would have kept it," he said. "I cannot believe you found it."

"Yvonne, tomorrow morning will you go with me to the north end of the island?" he asked.

"Yes, of course, why do you want me to go?"

"You will see," he said. "I love you."

"I love you too," she said as he leaned in to kiss her.

"Are you ready?" Henry asked.

"Ready for what?" she replied.

"Ready to go to the Chatham County Courthouse to get a marriage certificate."

"Yes," she said smiling, "I am."

Henry said, "I've got to grab a couple of things," as he went into the guest bedroom.

She waited for him at the elevator door, then they went down to the garage. He walked over to the door of his convertible, opening it for Yvonne.

"Thank you," she said.

He walked around the car to get in. When he was settled, the garage door opened, engine running, he lowered the top, telling Yvonne a scarf was in the glove box if she needed it.

This was the best Tuesday in the history of Tuesdays, she thought, as they left the island. The coastal breezes were cool this morning, but in her heart, she could not have felt warmer.

Henry was briefly thinking over the course of his entire life, wondering what incredible thing he ever did for karma, the universe, or God to have brought Yvonne to him. He was sure there was nothing. When he paid the clerk for the license, he turned to Yvonne asking, "Where do you want to get married?"

"On the beach where I first met you," she answered in a very straightforward manner because she thought he ought to know the answer to that question. "That place is as important to me as it is to you." Henry realized from Yvonne's expression that the question really was ridiculous; they both lived on the beach and their first meeting was at that spot. Even though that was where his wife's ashes had been scattered, weddings and funerals usually happened in the same places anyway.

"Do you want to get married today? Or are there people you need to invite or call?" he asked. Yvonne was a bit surprised at that statement, so she told him to let her think about it while they had lunch.

"What about your kids?" she wondered if this question was out of place.

"I explained this to you before; marriage is not about children. Marriage is about you and I repairing the damage each has suffered that we cannot repair for ourselves. Damage that was only increasing with the passing of time," Henry replied. He didn't know if that was entirely true for her; she had been ten years without Nate, but it was certainly true for him.

"Both of us have had weddings before so our families can't be upset, critical, accepting, or condemning if we decide to just keep this all to ourselves. For a while at least, Yvonne, I don't want to share you with anyone."

She was still smiling at him and nodding in approval when he asked, "What would you like to eat?" The events of the morning left him feeling like not eating at all.

"Something light," she said, not sure what she wanted.

"There is a little Japanese place called Sakura on Waters Avenue..."

"Yes!" she interrupted him. "They have the best California Rolls. Sushi was perfect," she said. Just like Henry. She and Nate had been there quite often but she had not been there since Nate's death; *time to keep exercising those ghosts*, she thought.

As they were about to finish their meal, Yvonne looked at Henry. "It can't be today. The only person I want to be there is working."

"Who is that?" Henry asked.

"Pam," was Yvonne's reply.

"The crazy owner of the restaurant where you used to work?" he asked, hoping she would quit and not be put off by his question.

"She is incredibly special to me, Henry," Yvonne said in a very somber tone. "Except for her finding me on the pier, inviting me to work with her, and treating me like a daughter..." Yvonne stopped. "Yes, Pam must be there. And Chuck too," she continued.

"The bartender?" Henry asked with a look of complete shock on his face. "Why Chuck?"

"Because," she said with a smile that would have gotten her anything she wanted, "he is licensed to perform weddings." She laughed as she said that he had performed marriage ceremonies dozens of times on the deck of the restaurant.

Henry was speechless. "Ok," was all he could say. When his thoughts cleared up after this remarkable revelation, he asked, "So how about tomorrow?"

"It will have to be in the morning before they open for lunch," she answered. "We need to go there and tell them this evening; do you want to have supper there?"

"Call Pam and have her reserve that back table on the deck for us at seven fifteen," he asked.

"Why seven fifteen?" Yvonne asked.

"The sun sets at seven thirty-five," he reminded. Pam was shocked at Yvonne's request; she had never called in a reservation, A.J.'s Dockside normally didn't make reservations, and Yvonne knew that. "Why do you want a reservation?"

"I'll explain it to you when I get there tonight," was all she would say. "Oh, before I go, tell Chuck to be at the table with you."

Pam looked at her watch; it was one-forty-five. The suspense would be awful. *What in the world was wrong with Yvonne,* she thought. *Why didn't she say? And why did she need a reservation?* Whatever, no chance that table would not be ready. "Chuck," Pam ordered, "go put the chairs on table sixteen and tape it off."

"Why do you want me to do that?" asked Chuck.

"Because the waitresses have trouble lifting those chairs; you're a damn man so handle it," was her reply.

As her call ended, Henry said, "I've got to make a stop on Wilmington."

"For what?" she asked.

"A bride needs a bouquet," he smiled.

"What are we going to wear?" she asked him.

"The same things we had on yesterday," he laughed. "We hardly wore them, and they are still at my house…" he paused as his expression changed to one of complete satisfaction and devilment, "…except you will need new panties."

Her reply was short but ended the conversation. "Why?"

Chapter 15

Pam was in the kitchen when they arrived for their reservations. She was walking out when the hostess walked them to their table. As Henry pulled her chair out for Yvonne, making sure she was comfortable, Pam remembered what Chuck had said about him. She did remember this man. So few men were as well-mannered or they had all died off, but this relic of the past remained, and it was him seating his wife as well as standing if she left the table to go to the restroom that had marked her memory. He was also the asshole from a week earlier that had made Yvonne so upset. Why was she here with him? Then it all made sense. She was here with a man.

"Want to introduce me to your man friend?" Pam asked as she approached the table.

She was not the owner or a server to him now; she was a guest of his soon-to-be wife. So, as Pam approached the table and began to speak, Henry rose from his chair.

"My name is Henry," he said. "Good to meet you, Pam."

As Henry was introducing himself to Pam, Chuck arrived at the table not wanting to get secondhand information.

As soon as the introductions were over, Pam and Chuck sat down. Pam did not really know how to react to Henry holding her chair; her husband Alex, who was a retired fisherman, had all the manners of the shrimp he was retired from catching.

Yvonne did not know how to break the news to Pam, so she just asked if she and Chuck would meet her and Henry at her condo tomorrow at nine a.m.

Before Pam and Chuck's minds could process the request, Yvonne continued, "We are getting married tomorrow. Chuck, I want you to perform the ceremony, okay?"

Silence, shock, and stillness overcame both Pam and Chuck. This emotionally void woman, who for years had been completely removed from any human contact, was getting married; to the guy who sent her off in a panic. Their minds were thinking similar thoughts, but it was Pam who spoke up first.

"I have never seen you look like this before," she told Yvonne. "Whatever this man did or said, it was the right thing." Pam meant every word; Yvonne was thinking of something else as she was nodding in agreement.

"Sure, did happen fast," Pam said. *Wasn't all that fast,* Yvonne thought as a huge smile adorned her face.

Before she could continue, Chuck said, "I'll be glad to perform the ceremony, but I'm wearing shorts and sandals like I always do."

Yvonne said, "I don't care what you wear as long as y'all are there."

Pam said, "She only heard of something like this happening once before. Her mother knew a woman who was catching a train to Macon to visit her grandmother in nineteen forty-two when a handsome young man sat down beside her on his way to training for World War II. By the time the train arrived in Macon, they were engaged. But even they didn't get married till his training was over," Pam explained. Then she asked, "So I guess you won't be working this weekend will you, or any weekends in the future?"

"I know it is sudden," Yvonne offered. But, no she was not planning to work anymore.

Pam looked at Henry, saying, "You better bring her here to visit even if you don't eat."

Henry smiled, saying "That besides the best food on earth, her restaurant had served as a better treatment than any medicine or hospital ever had." Chuck was smiling and nodding.

Pam had no reply; her thoughts were filled with the evening she had brought Yvonne here for the first time. Like an injured animal, she had taken her in, providing her with a place to heal until she recovered enough to leave. It was now time for her to go, but Pam was sorrowful that she was leaving. She was not a woman who showed any emotion, so to hide her sadness she gave Chuck a smack on the arm, telling him to get everyone something to drink.

"You already know what everybody drinks," she said, acknowledging his talent.

Chuck came back with drinks. He had turned the bar over to a capable college kid they called Stuey who had been working there for six years. Chuck had always liked the fact that the kid was not in a hurry to join the real world, making a seven or eight-year experience out of a four-year degree. *Smart kid,* Chuck thought.

They sat there talking, drinking, and enjoying each other's company until well after ten. Finally, during a break in the conversation, Henry stood up to excuse himself and Yvonne for the night.

"Thank you both for everything," Henry said, shaking Chuck's hand, then hugging Pam while whispering in her ear, "Especially for saving Yvonne."

Pam had started to pat his back as soon as he embraced her, a polite southern way of saying let me go, but as his strong embrace held her and his words resounded in her mind, Chuck and Yvonne both saw something no person on Earth had seen for years. A tear streamed down Pam's face. Now she hugged him back until he released his hold. As she separated from Henry, Pam looked directly into Yvonne's eyes and said, "He's a keeper."

As Henry and Yvonne made their way out of the restaurant, Chuck turned to Pam to ask, "What did he say to make you cry?"

"It's none of your damn business," Pam scowled. "And if you run your old gossiping mouth to anyone, I'll fire you."

Chuck laughed as loud as he ever did, saying, "How the hell are you gonna fire me when you ain't never hired me to begin with?"

At that, they both laughed walking to close the restaurant as they had been doing for years, just like an old married couple preparing for bed.

When the elevator door closed, Henry took Yvonne's hand as they walked out on the deck. They did not sit; instead, they walked over to the railing watching the tide come in by the glimmer of starlight. The curiosity was killing Yvonne; she wanted to ask but, at the same time, did not want to seem like an old busybody.

"I've got to ask, what did you say to Pam?" Henry turned to Yvonne, pulling her tightly against his body before he said, "I thanked her for saving you." Yvonne reached her arms around his neck and pressed herself tightly against his body. Her kisses were filled with the kind of passion usually reserved for young lovers at the beginning of discovering each other. With each second of those kisses, Henry felt as if the slow progress of time was reversing, returning him to a time when the future was filled with possibilities. He had been married for thirty-three years the first time and while he was kissing Yvonne, he was praying for as many with her.

Gently, he placed Yvonne so that she was resting on the rail of the deck; his hand went up the back of her shirt as he undid the clasp of her bra. He slid his hands inside the sleeveless top she was wearing, pulling her straps out and down so she could lift her arms out before he reached up the front of her blouse, removing her bra the way she did, but the purpose was not the same. When the bra fell on the deck, her shirt was next; he kissed her chest with each button until he removed her top and relocated his kisses to her breasts.

She was pulling his shirt up as he kissed her nipples; he paused only to let the shirt pass over his head. He lowered her feet to the deck as they both began to undo the buttons on each other's shorts. They stood body against body, as the waves crashed against the jetty; they took turns kissing each other's chests, then necks, and lips until she finally implored him in a voice he already loved. "I'm ready, I'm ready, Oh my god, I'm so ready." He kicked the clothing into a pile for a place to sit her gorgeous ass. Then he got on top of her, continuing to kiss her. There was no need to position himself; he was fully aroused, and Yvonne had maneuvered her hips, guiding him to where she wanted him to go. Henry began slowly to pace himself, making sure Yvonne would finish before he did. What he did not know was Yvonne was almost there, wanting him to speed up. Rather than speak, Yvonne used a move Nate had taught her as a means of self-defense. Henry was more than capable of defending himself but was not prepared when Yvonne suddenly pinned his left leg with her right leg, pushed his left arm across her body while simultaneously pushing with her left arm and leg and exploding up with her hips.

"What the hell?" Henry said when he was suddenly on his back.

Smiling, she had him where she wanted him, so she let him know by the movements of her hips that she was indeed already there, begging, forcing him to join her. *Damn*, he thought, I love this woman and this time, no thoughts of washing his car could prevent Yvonne from getting her way. They were both climaxing, the waves crashing upon the rocks drowning their sounds of ecstasy, as they were becoming one with each other. Soon all that remained were the sounds of the waves; they were motionless, soundless, body upon body in an embrace neither wanted to break. Yvonne then did something that if he did not love her already would have shattered any resistance. It was the kind of thing only people in love can do.

She raised back up sitting on his stomach while she squeezed him out then with each motion spread their mutual affection all over his stomach and laughed. Now he was as much a mess as she was, and their clothes were going to need to be washed. Henry rose so that they were both sitting, her legs wrapped around his waist, and he began to kiss her again. She was totally surprised as he moved his hips over his feet and stood up while holding her.

Yvonne was pleading "No, don't," as he carried her to the shower. The water was cold. But as he held her kissing her so softly, the coldness of the water was forgotten and all that remained was this warm, wonderful man.

As usual, Henry toweled her off before using the towel on himself. Yvonne gathered their clothes and then turned to look back at him standing there toweling off his head, much as he had done the first time, she saw him naked on this deck. She thought about Karen's horse, wondering if he knew what he was missing.

Henry saw her smile and said she looked like the cat that just ate the canary.

"It was way better," she said.

He opened the door, and as she walked past him into the house, he said, "You are sinfully gorgeous, but not after tomorrow."

"And you are a love god, William Henry Morgan."

Again, she left him speechless. Now it was time for bedtime rituals and good night kisses. They were both soundly asleep before either of them had turned over twice.

Chapter 16

After only two nights of sleeping together, Henry learned something about Yvonne's morning routine. Her body was awake before her eyes or brain were fully alert, so she did not want to be touched before she used the toilet and brushed her teeth. The only response he was going to get to "Good morning beautiful" was a mumbled, barely intelligible "morning". This would be a busy morning so Henry started gathering everything he would need to take with him to Yvonne's condo. It would take them about an hour to make their preparations, putting everything in Yvonne's car before driving to her condo.

When Yvonne came out of the bathroom, she had finished her make-up and hair much as it had been their first night together except for the fact she had not put on any clothes yet.

Henry turned and stopped. "You look goooooooood," he said, drawing out the word good as if it had many vowels in it.

"How good?" was her reply?

Smiling, he said, "Good enough to eat."

"That will have to wait," she said, "and where is your white outfit?"

"I'm not wearing it today," he answered, "and that is why I wanted you to be there with me this morning."

Yvonne let that statement as well as its implications work its way through her mind. She did not respond, only going about putting on her clothes and gathering everything she would need. There was no more conversation until he opened her door for her.

"Thank you," she said.

"You're very welcome, beautiful."

As Henry got in the car, Yvonne looked at him but did not speak; her expression let him know she had questions. Then she started the engine and drove them to her condo.

Henry gathered everything from the car except for her dress; he let her carry it so he wouldn't accidentally drag it on the ground or steps. When they had placed everything in her bedroom, Henry opened his backpack and removed a paper bag. It was ten minutes to sunrise. Henry asked, "Are you ready to go?"

"Yes," was all she said.

He took her hand as they stepped onto the path that led from the condo, through the dunes, to the beach. Silently, they walked until he was at the place he had been standing that first moment she saw him, only now he was hers. Or was he? She knew he did not like to talk during the sunrise, and it was getting brighter; the sun would be appearing soon.

"What are you going to do with that outfit, burn it?" she asked.

How did she know there was a lighter and starter fluid in the bag, he thought, but only replied, "Yes."

Yvonne grabbed Henry's hands with the strength he did not know she possessed, almost as if he were about to plunge to his death and she was saving him. Her eyes were pleading, becoming moist with tears as she implored, "Please don't."

Before either of them could reply, something happened on the horizon that neither of them had ever seen or would ever see again. As the sun appeared, there was the most magnificent green glow at the tip of the sun. It was the color of her birthstone.

When it appeared, Henry called out his wife's name. "Virginia," he yelled. "I know that green glow is you." He was having difficulty saying his words. The conflict of sorrow and happiness warring inside of him as tears streamed down his face did not prevent him from continuing. "I'm so sorry for everything I ever did to hurt you and thankful to you for letting me know Yvonne is the woman you gave me your blessing to marry." Then, he turned to Yvonne, pointing at the green glow beginning to fade to yellow and spoke, "Yvonne. That was Virginia."

Yvonne was so overwhelmed that she just wrapped her arms around him as if it were the last time they would ever be together. An embrace that lasted until the sun cleared the horizon.

"Okay," Henry said.

"Okay what?" was Yvonne's reply.

"I won't burn it," he said smiling.

"Good," Yvonne replied, "we have nine more months of sunrises to go before that outfit is retired. I'm going to make sure you honor that vow or how can I expect you to keep a promise to me if you begin our life together by breaking your promise to Virginia?"

"All right then," he said as he immediately stripped off his clothes and put on the outfit.

Good thing no one was near, she thought. When he pulled the shirt down her thoughts continued. He did in fact look like he should be on the cover of a book. Virginia was right in choosing this for him. "Do you want coffee?" is what she asked instead.

Pam and Chuck were knocking on the door at ten till nine. Many years ago, Yvonne had given Pam a pass to the gate in case she needed her for any reason.

"Dang," said Chuck, "Y'all look good," as he entered the condo seeing Henry and Yvonne dressed for the ceremony. "If y'all ain't wearing shoes, then neither am I," he continued, kicking off his sandals.

Pam hugged them both agreeing with Chuck that they both, "cleaned up good."

Henry handed Chuck a piece of paper with his and Yvonne's full names on it.

Chuck looked at it for a couple of seconds and handed it back. "I don't need that," he said.

Soon they were standing on the beach as Chuck looked at them both he began.

"Dearly beloved, we are gathered here today, in the presence of..."

Yvonne was aware of Chuck speaking, but all that mattered to her at this time was Henry. She had never believed in a million years there would be a man who could heal her shattered heart and then fill it to overflow with his love.

"I Do," Yvonne said.

A man who was not afraid of his emotions and capable of communicating his exact feelings without fear or concern for the consequences. He was the most confident self-aware man on the face of the earth; she was certain of that.

"I Do," Henry said.

"Then by the power vested in me by the State of Georgia, I pronounce you husband and wife, you may ki..." Chuck did not finish. "Y'all need to get a room," is what he said instead.

"I want Waffle House," Pam said loudly, not too big a price to pay for dragging me out here.

At that statement, the kiss was interrupted by laughter.

"Sounds good to me," Chuck agreed.

As they began to leave the beach, Henry turned and said, "Mrs. Yvonne Nichole Morgan. It has a nice ring to it."

"Yes, it does," she smiled while offering him a kiss.

"After breakfast, I have somewhere I want us to go," Yvonne said.

He knew where she wanted to go, Bonaventure, the cemetery where Nate was buried. He could do that without any problem. Henry was going to be cremated and hopefully thrown into the ocean with Virginia. But, if there was a place on earth where he could see himself being buried, it was there.

Breakfast was filled with excellent conversation and laughter, but mostly the joy a group of people have in experiencing the most notable events in life. When the server brought the check, Pam would not let Henry have it.

"I got this," she said, a wedding token. "Y'all come by at supper time, I have a real present for you."

Yvonne said, "You don't have to do anything like that, just you being here was all I needed."

"Honey, hush, I am a grown-ass woman and I do what I want, don't tell me what to do. Just come by."

At that, they all erupted with laughter as they left the diner.

"Do you know where we are going?" Yvonne asked Henry.

"Not the exact spot, but yes," was his reply.

As they left, Yvonne told Henry to pull into the pharmacy.

"What's wrong?" Henry asked.

Yvonne looked at him as if that were the dumbest question ever asked, "Mother Nature has arrived," she stated.

Damn, Henry thought, a helluva day for her to show up.

Yvonne did not know how she had forgotten this. She was as regular as the moon. Her periods had never been heavy so all she needed were tampons. When she came out, Henry was waiting at her door. *I am going to enjoy getting used to this,* she thought.

When they arrived at the cemetery, Yvonne told him the military part of the cemetery was in the back towards the river. Henry drove until Yvonne said, "This is the place." As they got out, Yvonne pointed to an unremarkable grave,

Nathaniel Wayne Bennett

Born March 8, 1977

Died September 15, 2010

Captain U. S. Army

Purple Heart Silver Star

Neither of them broke the silence until Henry said, "He was way too young. I was married as long as he lived. Y'all looked good together," he continued looking at the wedding photo medallion that was attached to the stone.

"Yes," to everything, was her wistful reply, "I just wanted you to see this."

"Is the spot next to him for you," Henry asked.

"It is," she replied, "even though he is not there."

Henry looked out over the cemetery and said, "None of them are," he touched his chest saying. "They are here," then he touched his temple, "and in here." Then before he walked away, he reached into his pocket and left a penny on the gravestone.

Chapter 17

Once they returned to Henry's house, their house, the plan for the day was simple, change into the most comfortable clothing they had and sit on the deck. The weather was perfect, sunny, and warm, not hot, and the breeze coming off the ocean was only enough to keep the sand gnats away.

"If I remember correctly, you asked the last question so it's my turn." Yvonne broke the silence.

"I think that game is over," Henry replied, "it ended when you made me marry you," he said, laughing.

"Oh, no it isn't, you asked me about where I lost my virginity but, I never got to ask you."

He thought the look on her face was exquisite "When his reply was, which time?"

What the hell was he talking about, she thought, *this was not something that could happen over and over.* The first time, she said:

"Well, he started; it was the fall of the year I turned nine years…"

"NINE! She yelled, no way in hell. This is supposed to be the truth."

"Do I get to tell you without a million interruptions or not," he asked, "and I swear to you that every word I say is the truth," So help me God!" As he made the motions, he was sworn to testify.

"I'm calling bullshit on nine," she said, "but continue."

He was a little surprised she knew that card game. *Keep that in mind for future reference,* he thought, before returning to his story, "It was the fall of the year I turned NINE!" He said with emphasis.

She was shaking her head in disbelief but not interrupting.

"The first year of elementary school meant a new school, but more importantly, new playground equipment..."

"What does playground equipment have to do with the answer to my question," she said?

Realizing she was not going to stop interrupting he just continued.

"...so, the swings on the elementary school playground dwarfed the swings at primary school and every boy ran as fast as he could at the beginning of recess to get a swing. These were at least ten feet tall so you could get incredible height before jumping out... He held up his hand to get her not to interrupt. ...but if you were not one of the fastest boys, the six swings would be occupied so you had to do something to occupy your time after calling seconds or thirds. The time killer of choice was climbing the support poles of the swings. This happened every day like clockwork until one day, and I don't recall if I did it first or if one of my friends, we began climbing on top of the poles instead of underneath. He held up his arm to show her the angle of the supports so that she got a clear picture. It was my second or third time climbing the pole and as I reached the top, the feeling I was experiencing was one pure rapture, every component of orgasm except ejaculate. A wet spot on my jeans in that location would have meant humiliation. When it subsided, the rapture was replaced by an incredible feeling of calm."

"That's not losing your virginity," Yvonne laughed.

"Perhaps it isn't or perhaps it is," Henry continued. "But I had a sexual relationship with that swing, as I am sure other boys did, dang that swing set was a brothel; until we broke up at the end of sixth grade."

Yvonne was laughing harder now but managed to ask why they broke up.

"Junior High School was on another campus," he explained. "And there were no swings."

So, she said between fits of laughter. "A man losing his virginity is a progression".

Now she was laughing uncontrollably.

Henry waited until she gathered herself and said. "Yes."

This only made his tale funnier as she returned to laughing.

"What happened in Junior High?" She asked. "A merry-go-round?" Her question served only to increase her laughter.

"Ha!" He said. "It wasn't at school smarty pants, it was in the bathroom of my parent's house."

As she began to just occasionally giggle, He said. "Do you remember when I told you about puberty arriving in my thirteenth year?"

She nodded as he continued, "Well that was not all that arrived. Many of the boys at school, mostly older boys would brag that they were now growing pubic hair and 'choking the chicken.' Well, I knew about the hair, but the other part was a complete mystery. I don't know why but, one day in the bathroom, the answer to my question would arrive."

"What question," she asked?

"Masturbation. The mystery would be solved," he laughed as he said.

"Somehow in my mind, it had something to do with the up-and-down motion on an erect penis. The pictures of women I had looked at in magazines made me believe a vagina must be soft and smooth. At this point, I had no idea that a firm grip of the hand could do the trick. As it turned out, my mother…"

Yvonne laughingly interrupted. "That's kind of Oedipal isn't it," her laughter exploding.

"…had a pair of fuzzy house slippers. Again, he had to pause for Yvonne's laughter. When I placed them on either side of my penis and began to slide them up and down, nothing was happening."

"Were you standing, sitting, or lying down?" Yvonne asked.

"I don't know the relevance of that but, just to satisfy your curiosity I was standing. At any rate, I was about to stop when a familiar old feeling from the third grade began to build. Instead of stopping, I began to move them faster and squeezed them firmer against my penis, which was a mistake."

"Why?" Asked Yvonne.

"When I was finished, there was a friction burn on the head of my penis."

His story came to a complete stop. She was now crying and heaving with bursts of uncontrollable laughter.

"Stop." She spoke. "Stop. I can't hear anymore."

"Oh no, he said you're gonna hear the entire sordid tale."

"As I was saying, I began to slide them faster until, voila! For the first time, semen was released, and Oh my! Did it feel good! I wasn't sure about many things but, I knew my penis worked. It was now very sore, and I had a mess to clean up. I wanted to shout the news to the universe but, deep down, I knew this would remain a secret forever."

Yvonne gathered her thoughts, so let me see if I got this progression: "Swing set, bathroom, Volkswagen. All that is left is the answer to my question."

"Philosophically," Henry said. "It is not the destination, Yvonne but, alas it is the journey."

"She was a girl whose name I cannot remember, in a hotel room of no consequence off post at Ft Jackson, South Carolina when I got leave at the end of basic training. There were no fireworks, no need for celebration, just a wham, bam, thank you, ma'am. To be honest, I enjoyed the swing set more."

From the smile on his face, she could tell his story was true. Yvonne's laughter was completely stopped. *How sad,* she thought.

This man was incredible. If there was a story in her past like his, there is no way on earth she could tell it. "Why did you tell me all that," she asked, fully grasping his embarrassment and her feelings of guilt for having laughed.

"You asked," he replied. "I will never lie to you," he swore. "Besides, the ending of the story is the answer to your question. The story is good but the ending sucks. Just to complete the question from the other night, there was the girl in the Volkswagen, at Ft. Jackson, one at Ft Bragg, a prostitute in Egypt, a chance encounter, and the girl from college, none of which have a name that I can remember. If I could redo my life that is one thing I would change. I wish I had waited to have sex with Virginia. There a very few certainties in life but this is one area where you can be absolutely certain. I will never cheat on you. EVER!" After a brief pause while looking into her eyes, he continued. "Okay, I know that you had only had sex with Nate, so what made you decide you would have sex with me?"

Her face turned a bright shade of red. "When I saw you in the shower that morning."

"Damn," he said. "If I had known that I would have postponed that refrigerator project."

"I'm glad we waited" she said. "The day we made love was the most exciting day of my life, except for my first wedding. But if I must be honest the sex was incredibly better with you. The anticipation of that night was exceptional, and your performance was magnificent, especially when you kissed me goodnight."

I must admit he said, hearing you say I love you to me before I went to sleep was special.

I'm getting hungry, he said, let's go find out what Pam has for you.

Soon they were at the A.J.'s, seated, and ordered their food before Pam came out of the kitchen. She walked over to the table explaining she would let them finish their dinner before being a bother. Neither of them saw her approaching as the server cleared the table, so they were surprised when she sat down next to Henry and handed Yvonne an envelope.

Open it Pam, ordered.

As Yvonne opened the envelope, she realized what Pam had done.

I can't take this, she said.

Oh, hell yes you can, those tickets are non-refundable. Consider it as a wedding present and your severance package. I told you that you were like a daughter to me. One I never had. The simplicity of your wedding as well as the location were exactly what I would have wanted my daughter to enjoy.

Henry was looking at them both, what is it? He asked.

Yvonne took the tickets out of the envelope, an Alaskan cruise, she said. It leaves in two days.

Henry knew Pam was like him, when her mind was made up there were no second thoughts. He did not try to discuss this with her, instead, he simply put his arm around her shoulders, kissed her cheek, and said thank you.

I'm happy to do it for y'all she replied. If anyone deserves this, it is Yvonne.

Yvonne got up to give Pam a proper hug as well as thanks. The season on Tybee was over and so were many of the dinner guests, regular customers on the island, had already come and gone. Since it was slow, Pam just sat and talked with them during sunset. Soon, Chuck joined them as well.

Let me tell you what happened this morning Yvonne began. I've never seen anything like it. She went on to tell them about the green glow that morning and how it was an amazing green color like her birthstone.

Henry interrupted; you were born in August.

August 3, 1982, was her reply.

Henry was catatonic.

Pam offered that they really did not know each other very well.

I'll never forget your birthday, he said to Yvonne.

And why is that Pam asked.

That was my wife Virginia's fifteenth birthday, he said.

With that statement, they all looked at each other in complete amazement.

What are the chances of two random people having the same birthday, Yvonne asked. Thinking no one could know.

Less than one percent, Chuck said, in fact, it is zero-point twenty-seven percent. Everyone looked at Chuck in amazement. How and why could he know that? But no one asked or doubted him. The conversation contained no more revelations but lasted till all the customers had left and it was time to finish closing.

Y'all have fun and I want pictures, Pam said as they left.

Henry was glad they had walked to the A.J.'s, this meant they got to walk back holding hands. Yvonne was just as happy thinking how crazy it was that Henry had married two women born on the same day. She thought those percentages might even be too far out there for Chuck, like winning the lottery kind of numbers.

While she was thinking that Henry spoke up, I've never been on a cruise, never been to Alaska, or on a honeymoon. Where did you and Nate go? He asked.

We didn't go anywhere, she said, he only had three days' leave, so we spent it in the condo on Tybee.

Soon they were ready for bed, the good night kisses finished when Yvonne said what a bummer it was that they could not make love, on my wedding day of all days.

"Why can't we?" Henry, he answered.

"It will ruin the bed," was her reply, and besides Nate would never have sex with her during this time of the month, she told him.

He scooped her off the bed and he took her to the bathroom, "I'm not Nate and you won't ruin anything," he said, turning the water on in the shower.

She was surprised at how loud 'Oh my God' sounded in the bathroom.

Chapter 18

As they boarded the flight to Seattle, Yvonne took Dramamine while Henry opted for wine. She had never liked flying and was hoping sailing would be different. They were both sleeping when the captain announced they were beginning their descent to SEA/TAC International Airport. The shuttle took them to the Bell Street Cruise Terminal at Pier Sixty-Six where the ship was docked, just minutes till boarding, so they were taking in the view. A valet service took their bags from the airport directly to their balcony stateroom, which they were looking forward to seeing.

The name of the ship was Bliss, and they both thought it was perfect for their honeymoon. Everything was perfect except the weather. Shortly after the ship began its cruise, the fog rolled in, and neither of them had ever seen fog like this; it was like a thick cloud had descended, blocking all visibility. They could barely see anything from the balcony, even if the ocean was out of view. Fortunately, they both felt like taking a nap after the flight, so the visibility would soon be zero anyway.

Around five that evening, Henry asked Yvonne what she wanted to do. Surprisingly, there were a variety of options. For the next two days, they just enjoyed each other's company, talked, and took shore excursions to shop, all the while hoping the weather would break.

It took a couple of days for Henry's internal clock to reset, but on day three, he was back on schedule. When he woke, the sun was beginning to light up the sky over the mountains. He kissed Yvonne's neck, whispering for her to wake up.

She saw nothing as she went to the bathroom to take care of her morning routine, and when she emerged, she smilingly asked Henry if he brought the beach outfit since it was sunrise.

He chuckled, explaining he was a southern boy, and that outfit would not do in this cold. He would be wearing a fleece warm-up with a wool coat, suggesting she do the same. Or he said, as he laughed harder, "Your nipples might put my eye out."

They dressed quickly and then opened the curtains and balcony doors to take in the view the sunlight was beginning to reveal. If the weather had to pick only one day to break, they agreed, this was the day they would have picked. The view of Glacier Bay was beyond either of their abilities, or for that matter anyone else who had ever witnessed this sight, to put into words. The air was so crisp, cold, and fresh that their nostrils tingled at the first breath. Neither of them was speaking; their eyes were saturated with visions of this incredible place. Their breath was creating a fog of their making with each exhale. Henry could feel ice forming on his mustache, and he was thinking the incredible color blue in the glacier was the same as Virginia's eyes, eyes that were closed forever. He closed his eyes for a moment, wishing they could have done this before she left him.

Yvonne was also thinking of Nate; he had been sent on a temporary assignment for Arctic Weather Training. Upon returning, he had said how incredible Alaska was and that one day they would have to go. That day never came.

They just stood there holding each other, comforted by the thoughts that each of them would have rather been here with someone else, but the grief of that knowledge was comforted by the person they were with on this ship; Bliss.

The name was perfect.

What broke their thoughts of longing was the breaching of a humpback whale.

They both yelled, "Wow!" as the huge mammal left the water, returning with a tremendous crash, thrilled that this would be an experience they would share forever.

"I'm glad you're here with me," Henry said, pulling Yvonne closer.

"There is no place I would rather be," she said. As she kissed him, she felt the ice in his mustache, remarking they should go back inside.

The photo they took of themselves with Glacier Bay in the background would eventually be enlarged, framed, and placed on the mantle above the gas logs in their home. They had taken it just after the whale had wiped away the memories of loss, immediately replacing them with exhilaration; it was that expression of youthful exuberance which made the photo compelling. Henry was not a particularly jealous man, but the reason he loved this photo and would never express it to anyone was that the ring on Yvonne's hand was not Nate's.

Yvonne had embraced Henry in the exact same manner Virginia had in every photo she had seen of them together. She understood exactly how Virginia must have felt in every photo he had in the guest bedroom; secure and loved. Except for the one day at Glacier Bay, they both felt the cruise had been a bit of a letdown. The ship, the crew, the food, and the excursions were all great, but the weather was horrible. After a life spent in sunny Georgia, they both agreed neither of them could ever live in a place as gloomy as the Pacific Northwest. A great place to visit they agreed but not to live.

Their plane home was departing in a couple of hours. Henry was restless, so Yvonne asked him what was wrong.

"Are you ready to go home?" he asked.

She could tell by the tone of his voice as well as the fact that he asked the question that he was not.

"Not particularly," she replied.

Henry smiled; "I'll be back in a minute." He walked to refund the airline tickets and then reserved a rental car.

"Where are we going?" She asked.

"Whatever destination you put in your phone's GPS," was his answer. "I am chauffeuring the bride on her honeymoon."

"I've always wanted to go to Wyoming," she said.

"Ok, Jackson Hole and Yellowstone it is." As she was putting the destination in her GPS, he remembered the first time he had been to those places. There were pictures of him and Virginia on the deck of the Lodge overlooking Jackson Lake with the Grand Tetons in the background. That had been their first vacation since they became empty nesters. The only argument they had in ten days had been his reluctance to spend more time at Yellowstone. He hated the crowds, traffic, and they had not seen a single animal except for deer. She had wanted to see a bear or buffalo and begged him to stay longer, became angry, and pouted when he would not. This time he would stay as long as Yvonne wanted.

The weather for the entire trip was fantastic. A little snow in Montana but, nothing treacherous around Glacier National Park, blustery at the Badlands and Mount Rushmore, then just nothing, no remarkable weather, no sights, just a boring highway. They took turns driving, napping, and looking for points of interest as they made their way toward St. Louis.

They were both tired and achy after driving from South Dakota through Iowa and into Missouri. The hotel was not one either of them would normally have chosen but it seemed to be in a safe place, and they just wanted to be out of the car.

Two men were drinking in the lobby as they were completing the paperwork for their room. It was obvious they were checking out Yvonne while sputtering vulgarities in a muffled voice but loud enough for them to hear. One of the men asked the other how much he thought a night with her costs. But, in a tone and choice of wording that was better suited for the gutter. Henry asked Yvonne to finish signing them in while turning and taking two steps toward the man.

"I'll only ask you once to apologize to my wife," and Henry was interrupted.

"Your wife?" Blurted out the man with profanity laced into his comment. "What are you going to do about it, old man?" he said as he started towards Henry.

His friend also stood up to join in or at least show solidarity with his rude, vulgar friend.

Yvonne did not speak, she had seen Henry in his workout room punching his heavy bag, so she knew when he stepped back slightly with his right foot while bringing his open hands up in front of his chest, exactly what was about to happen.

The drunk thought Henry was backing away from him so when Henry asked him to please not come any closer, he began to say what he was going to beat out of Henry.

His mouth had only begun to form the first letter of that word when with a speed and power completely unexpected by either of the men. Henry landed a straight left to the center of the drunk's face. Blood immediately exploded with the sound of the impact of the punch, and the drunk's forward momentum immediately reversed with him falling back onto the floor.

Stunned, the second man put his hand in his pocket removing a knife as he said he was going to cut Henry.

The tone and tenor of Henry's speech was one she had never heard before; he looked squarely at the man and explained. "If you try, I will break your arm and shove that knife up your ass," Henry warned. After a pause of only seconds, Henry continued, "Put that back in your pocket and help your friend."

It was apparent that a combination of the punch, its result, and Henry's obvious capabilities which rattled in the drunk's head, along with what was most assuredly a promise rather than a threat, resulted in a moment of clarity not usually present when alcohol is involved, so the man did as he was told.

Yvonne asked the clerk for a bag of ice before they went to their room. Henry did not speak, instead, he followed Yvonne without pausing or complaining as she opened the door for them. He sat in the only chair in the room as she washed the blood off his hand before applying the ice pack.

He was sitting in the chair; however, his mind was continuing the action in the lobby. The drunk, whether he lunged to stab or swung to slash was about to find that his attack would be turned into a sudden vicious takedown. The stab would have resulted in Henry catching his wrist pulling him forward then barring his arm for a slam onto the floor, his shoulder would not be able to resist the upward twisting of his arm resulting in a break or dislocation. Or as the slash passed, he would have stepped forward bear hugging this drunk while hip-tossing the hell out of him before putting his legs across the drunk's head and chest while pulling the drunk's arm with both of Henry's hands on the drunk's wrist, again resulting in a break or dislocation. He was about to insert the man's knife when...

"Hey," Yvonne broke his concentration, "are you okay?"

"I will be soon," Henry said.

"It has been twenty minutes already," Yvonne responded. "I've already brushed my teeth, so why don't you do the same and get into bed with me?"

"Yes, ma'am," Henry answered.

Usually, Henry began his dance with sleep on his back. After their goodnight kisses, he remained on his left side holding Yvonne close, the way a small boy cuddles a teddy bear. What he whispered into her ear, she knew, was not a meaningless comment but a vow.

"Before anyone could ever touch or harm you, they would have to kill me," he said before kissing her neck and laying his head on his pillow.

Yvonne did not reply. It wasn't necessary.

They spent the next day in St. Louis doing the whole tourist itinerary before driving to Metropolis, Illinois to spend the night. Metropolis, the home of Superman, the sign said. The photo they took in front of the twenty-foot-high man of steel would find its way to a spot behind Chuck's bar. Chuck loved Superman.

The next day they drove to Tybee. They both needed the ocean waves and breezes to restore their souls.

Chapter 19

Their honeymoon had lasted for almost three weeks; it was now the fifth of November, and Thanksgiving was only eighteen days away. So far, only Pam and Chuck knew of the wedding. Neither Henry nor Yvonne had mentioned it to their families; this would be a surprise to them all at dinner. It had not been difficult to keep their marriage quiet; their families knew their grief so an occasional check-in would do the trick. Tomorrow was a problem; it was his daughter's birthday, and she was expecting him for dinner. The big three-oh, thirty. To him, it was the first birthday of adulthood. He was out of ideas; Yvonne was no help either so as they explained the dilemma to Pam while showing her their photos, she smiled.

"Handsome, don't worry about it. Just tell them to meet here, I'll make sure there is only one open table so that when a lonely lady comes in, I'll ask if y'all mind if she sits with you. You tell me it is your daughter's birthday, so I'll look at her. If she is anything like her father, she won't object."

Henry smiled at the deviousness of the idea. He wanted Yvonne to be there just hoping his quick-minded daughter would just try to hook them up and not see they were already together. Henry knew his daughter would suspect something though; there was no way he could express the sadness or remorse of his former self. Yvonne had changed him. Saved him. Henry and Yvonne were at the bar when the hostess escorted Elaine and Ryan to the table. After they were all seated, and had ordered their drinks and food, Pam came up to close the deal. When the request became Elaine's decision, she said, "Of course she could join us."

Elaine noticed how her father was sneaking looks at Yvonne but what she did not see was Yvonne rubbing her feet on Henry's legs under the table. Pam brought out the cake after their meal while the entire staff came to sing Happy Birthday. Henry handed her an envelope with the same present he had given her for half her life, a piece of silky paper with an engraving of Benjamin Franklin. Elaine said thank you, and that something about him looked different. Knowing they were about to leave, Yvonne excused herself to the restroom thanking them for their hospitality, allowing her to enjoy their celebration instead of eating alone. As she left, Elaine looked at her father and said, "What are you waiting for? She likes you, ask her out."

Henry stopped smiling, explaining a young woman like that has no interest in an old man like me. As they all walked out, Elaine and Ryan got in their car. Henry said good night, "I forgot something, see y'all at Thanksgiving." If they had been slower leaving, they would have seen a couple emerge from the restaurant, holding hands and then kissing. "What did your daughter say when I left the table?" Yvonne asked.

"She said I should stop waiting and ask you out because in her eyes you liked me," he answered. "Smart girl," Yvonne replied, "do you realize I am only eight years older than her?" "You're only seven years older than my son," Henry said smiling. "I am a cradle robber."

The thought then entered Yvonne's head and quickly made it to her mouth where it escaped as a revelation. "I am a stepmother," she shrieked. "Not only that," Henry added, "but sometime around your next birthday you are going to be a grandmother," he laughed as he said.

"What!" She screamed. "How long have you known that?" "Since the day we met after the storm," he answered. With more than a tinge of anger she asked, "And when were you going to tell me?"

Henry stopped and wrapped his arms around her while focusing his attention entirely on her eyes. "To be honest, someone has been a serious distraction lately, and I only just remembered it myself." While the answer was processing in her brain, the reality of what he had just said sank in deeper. "I am going to be a grandmother."

"I'm too young to be a grandmother," she whimpered as she replied to him. As she said that another thought completely removed any thoughts of anger at Henry. She would get a baby, a grandbaby but a baby, nonetheless. Any thoughts of children or the hope of them had long since died and been buried, but now this man was giving her everything she ever imagined she had wanted and more. Happiness, she had never known was washing over her, baby clothes, diapers, Christmas at grandma's house, decorations, parties… it was too much.

She started running towards the house; it was not much further for them and to his surprise he could not catch her. Yvonne was removing her clothes as she was entering the house. As he entered the house she yelled from the bedroom, "Hurry up husband, your wife has something for you."

Henry had caught her and joined her on the bed. Yvonne quickly had her way with Henry, and he was thankful for her enthusiastic present. "You forgot the towel," he said when they were finished, lying side by side in the bed. "Then we'll change the sheets tomorrow, you know how to do laundry," she laughed.

When he could finally think about what to say, he responded to her comment about the sheets. "Indeed, I do know how to do the laundry and for what you just did I will gladly become an old washerwoman."

"Old washer man," she corrected him, "or washer stud," she corrected herself. As she said that she thought back over the last eighteen days. The only day they had not made love was the night he punched that drunk. When her breathing slowed, she turned to him and said, "I thought older men only had sex once or twice a month."

"I've read that crap too," he said, "I don't know who they survey but, the average would be higher if they asked me."

"If I can ask," she timidly spoke, "how often did you and Virginia have sex?"

"You nor anyone else would believe me but, probably somewhere around two to three times a week. The day before she died in fact."

"My turn," he said, "how often did you and Nate have sex?"

"Less than half of that easily," was her reply. "He was deployed three times and always training, so many lonely nights. And I believe you."

"Well, I will do my best to keep you caught up," he smiled.

"I'm not sure if you can," she teased.

"Well, the sheets are already ruined, so why don't we go for two?" he asked.

Yvonne pulled him on top of her as she was kissing him. The sound she made while kissing him was all the motivation he needed.

"Um hem!"

They lay there motionless on the bed, him on his back, her arm and leg over him, their breathing beginning to synchronize.

"You're going to have to do something about that screaming," he said, "when the grandkids are here, you'll wake them up," he smiled while kissing her forehead.

"Do really want me to?" was her reply? "I don't think I can. I would explode if I tried to hold that inside me."

"It drives me wild," he said, "I just wish it would last longer."

"Any longer," she said with no smile at all, "would just be exercise or kill me. You always seem to finish as I can't take it anymore."

"That's what makes me finish," he said, "my mother always taught me, ladies first."

"I don't think your mother taught you that," she said.

"No, Virginia did," he said, "you and she are exactly alike in bed, except you are a younger version, and louder."

Yvonne then asked, "Do you ever think about her while we are making love?"

"I swear by everything I love that I do not," Henry begged. She could see in his eyes he was telling her the truth.

"Have you ever thought about Nate?"

Her answer sent them both to dreamland. "HA! Ha! NO!"

Chapter 20

For the next couple of weeks, they began to develop a daily routine of walks on the beach followed by breakfast, visits to antique shops, or short drives around Savannah. If it was raining, more than likely they returned to bed, sometimes falling back to sleep, and sometimes sleep only came after…

The preparations for Thanksgiving were all made. Henry already had an excuse for not being there as the guests arrived, so his daughter would be there to greet them. She also had final preparations to make for the dinner, and she loved her dad's kitchen.

Henry had taken his truck to Yvonne's condo where they would wait for Elaine's call letting them know everyone was present. This would be a small gathering: Henry's children, Yvonne's parents, Karen, Pam, and Chuck. He thought his son would be the last to arrive since they were driving in from Commerce. He was thinking about the guests when something crossed his mind; he had not told Yvonne.

"I haven't told you this before, but there is something about my son you need to know," Henry said with a very solemn face.

They were sitting on her balcony and had just been discussing dinner while having their coffee. Yvonne was surprised by this sudden announcement.

"What's wrong?" she said.

"My son is a disabled veteran," he explained. "He joined the Army in two thousand nine, serving in an engineering unit with the Second Infantry Division out of Ft. Lewis."

As he spoke, old pain visited Yvonne; she knew this was not a happy story and her own experiences made it worse.

"Was it an IED?" she asked.

"Two," Henry replied.

"The first one hit the vehicle in front of him."

"It wasn't a Humvee," she said, horrified.

"No, the vehicles they were in were exceptionally large Maxx Pros with mine detection equipment and fifty-caliber machine guns."

Yvonne's face showed relief that it was not a Humvee; the idea his son could have witnessed her husband's death was mortifying.

"The explosion was such that the Maxx Pro in front was destroyed along with the four-man crew."

"He saw that?" she asked.

"The blast from the device shook his vehicle. Unfortunately, he was the gunner in the turret on the top of the vehicle and was concussed from the explosion. About three weeks later," he continued, "his vehicle hit a smaller device. This time the vehicle turned over on its side, and the other members of the crew had bumps and bruises, but for my son, it was the equivalent of being body slammed from about twelve feet. He remembered being slammed, but the impact of the vehicle rolling over broke the mount for the fifty-caliber machine gun, and it crashed into his head."

Yvonne was stunned.

Henry continued; he was unconscious for over twenty hours but was only diagnosed with a permanent brain injury more than a year later. He must take medication to control seizures.

"Why haven't you told me this before?" she asked.

"Well, it was ten years ago. Virginia and I were just so happy he came home. His injury paled in comparison to those parents whose sons did not come home or came home with worse injuries. I wanted you to know before you spoke with him so you would not have this shock. You needed to know he was medically retired from the military and is unable to work. That way a question about what he does for a living won't result in a painful answer."

Yvonne realized he had not told her because the topic had never come up. He did not speak often about his children or his family. He was telling her this now to keep her from being hurt, protecting her.

"Ok, is there anything else I need to know?" she stated more than asked.

"His wife is a naturalized citizen from Korea and is two and a half months pregnant."

"How about your brother and sisters?" she continued.

"I have two brothers and three sisters," he continued; "I am the fifth of six." He told her about all the spouses and their children and the fact that they all got along well but were seldom able to gather as a family. They all had prior commitments this year, he said, so none of them would be here.

"Do you think they will like me?" Yvonne asked.

"I'm kind of a black sheep," he stated, "they all know that I have been traveling my own path since I could walk, so it would not be a shock at all to them that we got married the way we did, and yes, they will most definitely like you."

"Why wouldn't this be a shock?" she asked.

"I've done it before," was his reply.

She did not understand; he had only been married once so how was that even possible?

He saw the look on her face, so he began to explain.

"Virginia and I had been engaged for six months with a June wedding planned. I don't remember all the details of exactly why I got cold feet, but when the opportunity to go on an IRR assignment came in the mail, I jumped at it."

"What is the IRR?" she asked. Her knowledge of the military was much better than most people, but this was something new.

"The Individual Ready Reserve," he said, "processes paperwork. While serving at Ft. Bragg, I was cross-trained as a clerk because not many clerks want to serve in an Infantry Unit."

"The IRR wanted me to come to work through old files, so the military knew their budget for retirements and such."

"The only people who knew I left for St. Louis were my parents."

"You just left her," Yvonne said, in a very disapproving tone.

"After a week in a lonely hotel room, the realization of a life without her settled all my doubts. So, I called my mother asking her to fly Virginia to St. Louis where we could get married."

"What did your mom say?" she asked before he could continue.

"Laughing," he said, "she told me planes flew to Atlanta just like they did to St. Louis. I could fly home because she was not missing my wedding."

"So, you flew home," she said.

"I wish you could have known my mother," he said, "very seldom did she not get her way."

"While I was planning to fly home, my mother got into gear to prepare for a wedding. My two brothers, none of my sisters, and my wife's parents were in attendance."

"Where did the ceremony take place?" she asked.

"In the living room of my parent's house."

"Wow, did everyone think y'all were pregnant?" she asked.

"I'm sure most people suspected that was the reason Virginia and I had married in such a hurry, but when our son was born almost three years later, those thoughts were put to bed."

"Is there anything I need to know before I meet your parents?" he asked.

"My dad's name is Harold, and my mom's name is Vivian, but everyone calls her Bibi." He was thinking how that could be when Yvonne said, "there is no reason."

"Oh," he said, "no family member calls my son anything but Bubba."

Before she could ask, he said, "my daughter could not say brother," then the phone rang.

"Are you ready for this?" Henry asked.

"To let everyone know that you are my husband," she said, almost looking through him, "I am ecstatic. But I am worried about my parent's reactions. You are only two years younger than my mother and five years younger than my father."

"So, you're saying I'm old," he laughed, and she smacked his arm.

Chapter 21

Henry called his daughter, who did not believe his story about dessert. She wanted to know why he was not there.

"Get everyone seated at the table but leave the seat next to him open," Henry said.

"Why?" was her reply?

"Because I said so," he laughed as he said. He was laughing because that answer had not worked at any time in his daughter's life.

Before Elaine ended the call, he could hear her telling everyone to be seated. She had never accepted that response, but she knew he was not going to answer her question either.

From the steps leading to the deck and then the front door of their house, they could hear everyone talking.

It was finally time.

When Henry opened the door, walking in and holding Yvonne's hand, everyone stopped talking, turning to see them enter. Henry pulled Yvonne's chair, positioned near the end of the table between him and her mother. Once Yvonne was seated, Henry continued to stand and asked everyone to bow their heads.

"Henry gave thanks for the meal, those whose hands prepared the food, those who would consume the food, and the God who provided it, then he thanked God for the most beautiful, compassionate, and loving woman who rescued him from the depths of despair, his wife Yvonne. Amen."

Usually, the response at southern Thanksgiving blessing would be a smattering of "Amens" from those who were in agreement, but there was almost a simultaneous gasp.

Pam, Alex, and Chuck started clapping, so everyone snapped out of their shock and joined in. Two people at the table joined in with noticeable reluctance: Yvonne's father and Henry's son.

Although the meal was filled with questions for them both, Henry asked Yvonne if she would speak with Bubba, and he would speak with her father after the meal.

During the meal, Yvonne answered a thousand questions from her mother. There was only a slight question in her mind about this man because she could tell from Yvonne's responses that she loved him very much, and for the first time in a decade, her daughter was alive again. Bibi and Yvonne had spent less and less time together over the years, even though she was her only child. Bibi's face always expressed sympathy, something Yvonne hated; Yvonne was always angry.

When they finished eating, Bibi asked if she would like to get together for Black Friday.

Yvonne let that question sink in before looking at her mother and saying yes; they had not done that since Nate's death.

They were both crying as they hugged, then Yvonne excused herself to go speak with Bubba.

Yvonne asked him if he would join her in Henry's workout room, so he followed her.

As Yvonne left the room with Bubba, the women all seemed to congregate, telling each other about how that news affected them and sharing stories about their past experiences. The men went to the front deck and pretty much did the same thing.

Henry introduced himself to Harold, who told him to call him Harry.

Henry asked, "Would you like something to drink, bourbon or brandy?"

Harry replied, saying he thought a brandy would help.

This time Henry filled the glasses to the top sail on the schooner, thinking this conversation might take a while and the brandy would be in the house but they would be on the roof.

Harry followed Henry to the stairs leading to the roof. "This is really a nice place you have here," he said.

"Thanks, I've not been in it long," he said.

They stopped near the loungers but after the meal they just had, both men chose to stand.

Harry looked at Henry and said, "Tell me what happened?" in a manner that indicated someone had died.

Instead of beginning his story with the day on the beach, Henry began his story with the day Virginia died. Harry could see the same expression on Henry's face that he had seen on his daughter's face for the past ten years. That expression completely changed to one of incredible joy as soon as he mentioned meeting Yvonne on the beach.

Harry stopped him, "How old are you?" he asked.

"I'm fifty-seven," he said.

"Don't you think that is a bit old for my daughter?" he asked.

Henry asked him if he saw any difference in Yvonne at dinner today.

"I must admit," Harry said, "we haven't had Thanksgiving Dinner together since Nate was killed."

"Did she look happy?" Henry asked.

"She looked happier than I've seen her in years," Harry said.

"I love your daughter," Henry said, "and if I could change things, she would be having dinner at your house with Nate and Virginia would be here with me. None of us know how long we have to enjoy this life, so I hope you'll accept that my intention is to love Yvonne until death parts us."

"I would just hate to see her get hurt again," Harry said.

"So would I," Henry replied, "think I'll stay around a while to be sure."

Then they both began to ask and answer questions about each other, past experiences, and life in general. When Henry explained why he had been on the beach that day, Harry became visibly upset that he had cheated on his first wife, even though it was thirty-three years ago; to him, it was today.

"Don't ever do that to Yvonne," he stopped talking but, in his mind, the sentence continued, "or you will have to deal with me." That was how the sentence ended. The problem was he could see Henry was physically a much stronger man than he, and if he tried to deal with him, there would be an undesirable result. The expression on Henry's face let Harry know his evaluation was correct.

Yvonne and Bubba were alone in the workout room. "Who are you?" he asked.

Yvonne began by explaining her husband had been killed in Afghanistan at the same time he was there.

"What unit was he in?" Bubba asked.

"He was in the Third ID," she said, using jargon she knew he understood.

"What was his MOS?" he asked.

"He was an Infantry Officer but, on this deployment, he was the battalion S-2."

"How the hell did an S-2 get killed?" he exclaimed and immediately realized the inappropriateness of that question but, rarely did headquarters guys get killed and especially not officers. The expression on Yvonne's face told him he had hurt her, and he was immediately sorry.

"I didn't mean it that way," he said, "I just never heard of that happening before."

Yvonne said she agreed with him; it was only two or three weeks before the end of the deployment.

Bubba answered he had been hurt at about the same point in his deployment.

"How did you meet my father?" Bubba asked.

Yvonne began with the restaurant, describing how she reacted when he explained why part of the meal was left.

"That is what they always did," Bubba said, "my mom loved shrimp..." his voice cracked, and he began to cry. "I miss her so much," he said through tears.

Yvonne walked over to hug him, and much to her surprise, he hugged her tightly while his face was on her shoulder as he continued crying.

"It's not fair, she was supposed to be here to be my baby's grandma."

"I'm sorry," said Yvonne, realizing while her wounds were now covered with scars, his wounds were still bleeding.

"I promise to do the best I can to fill in for her," she replied.

He was surprised at her promise and looked into her eyes. Although Yvonne's eyes were brown, the expression of compassion was as real as any his mother ever showed.

"I could not have children," she said, "so I am looking forward to this baby as much as you are, probably more."

"My mom was the same way," he said, "she would have gone nuts for a grandbaby."

As they continued talking, interrupted intermittently by tears from them both, they began to form a relationship that would greatly strengthen them. Yvonne did not know that this was the first time Bubba had cried since his mother died; his wounds could now begin to heal.

"Finally," he said, "there is no way in hell a baby will ever be able to say, 'Yvonne, what is your middle name.'"

Yvonne was smiling as she said, "Nichole."

Neither of them knew it, but Bubba's yet unborn daughter would fasten her own name to Yvonne, one that she would hear as if it came from the angels themselves: Nina.

By the time they finished wiping their eyes, gathering themselves to rejoin the others, Henry and Harry were already down from the roof.

When all the questions had been answered, desserts eaten, hugs completed, and the last of the guests offered their thanks before leaving, only Bubba and Loni remained. Yvonne went to her purse to get something and handed it to Bubba.

"I'm not going to call you Bubba," she said, "I'm going to call you William."

"My mother called me William," he said, "I don't mind if you do. What is this?" he asked.

"It is the gate key along with the door key to my condo on the north side of the island," she explained.

William said he knew the place and thanked her for its use during their stay. It had not been that long ago he had dropped by to see his parents when they were not expecting them and been exposed to the sounds of his parents in the throes of passion. If Yvonne were anything like his mother he thought, the condo would keep that occurrence from ever happening again. They were newlyweds after all.

Henry and Yvonne were on the deck relaxing after the best Thanksgiving either of them had in a while, just enjoying the coolness of the evening. He was sitting in one of the chairs with his feet propped up, and she was lying curled up on his lap with her head on his shoulder. A blanket covered them both.

"That went better than I hoped," she said.

"I thought so too," he replied.

"Are you hungry?" she asked.

"You must be kidding," he said, "I couldn't eat another bite."

"Not even dessert?" she asked, kissing his cheek.

"I'm an idiot," he thought as he stood up with her in his arms.

"There is always room for dessert," he smiled.

"It can't be a marathon," Yvonne said, "I've got to get up early to go Black Friday shopping with my mother."

"I'm not making any promises," he said.

"The thought of a normal life returning for them both brought with it a feeling of completeness and contentment. He was glad she was going; his son would be there anyway so at least he didn't have to go."

"Would you mind inviting Loni to go with you?" he asked.

"After," she said.

This time he knew exactly what after meant.

Chapter 22

Yvonne had invited Elaine, Loni, and Karen to join her mother for Black Friday. Karen had an SUV, so they all went in her car. By the time everyone said goodbye, Yvonne was wiped out. This was not something she was used to, and the crowds, as well as all the conversations, had made her ready to be home. When she left her mother's house, she called to let Henry know she was on her way.

When she got back, Henry was waiting at the garage to help her with her bags.

"Did you get everything you were looking for?" he asked.

"Almost," was her reply.

"Well, it looks like you bought out every store in Savannah," he said, "I will have to make two trips."

Yvonne thought to herself if this was a condition that affected all men or just the ones she had known. Why does every man act as if two trips from the car are a calamitous defeat? She just picked up two boxes and went with him to the elevator. His arms were packed with things, and he would, in fact, have to make another trip; he would not let her do it.

When they got the bags to the guest bedroom, Yvonne looked at the photos; yes, she decided she would have photos just like that but in the living room. She knew which one she wanted most.

After putting the bags down, he took her by the hand, leading her to the bedroom.

"Where is William?" she asked.

"He went back to the condo to help Loni," he replied, "I'm sure she has as much crap as you do."

"Not crap, presents," she clarified.

"The same thing," he said.

Henry was a very unusual man, she thought; material possessions meant absolutely nothing to him. It was simple things that made him happy: good food, his 'libations' as he called them, and sex with her. She was fine with all three, but right now, she was tired. He reached around her effortlessly undoing and removing her bra. How does he know she thought? Instead of removing her clothes, he sat her on the edge of the bed and sat on the floor, taking off her shoes and massaging her feet. She was learning that he was meticulous about everything. Every part of each foot was ordered, by his hands, to release the tension and pain that built up throughout the day. As she was becoming sleepy, he stood up, taking her hands and pulling her towards him. Wow, she thought, my feet do feel better. Then he removed the rest of her clothes. Well, she thought, I do feel better, but instead of putting her on the bed, he carried her to the tub, filled with hot water and bubbles.

He touched her foot to the water while asking if it was too hot.

"No," she said, and he lowered her into the tub.

He knew she loved the smell of peppermint candles, and one was burning beside the tub, and soon there would be a hot cup of coffee beside it.

"I'll get the rest of your crap," he said.

"Thanks," she replied, barely able to speak at all. This was incredible. While she had been shopping, his thoughts had been about how she would feel when she returned. Not who she was with, what she was doing, how much money she was spending, it was all crap to him anyway. He had been focused on making her feel as good as he possibly could after what he knew would be a tiring day. Okay, she thought, he can call it crap if he wants to. In fact, she did not care what he said. It was what he did and was continually doing for her that mattered. The last thing she thought before falling into almost a complete sleep was that if all men were like Henry, divorce lawyers would be out of business. Her next thought was what in the world do you get a man for a Christmas present who clearly has everything he wants or desires? There was nothing.

Neither she, her mother, Pam, Karen, nor his daughters could come up with a single thing.

Henry had gone to Savannah while they were out; he knew exactly what he wanted to get for Yvonne. The jeweler said it would be ready by the twenty-first of December, which was okay as long as it was ready before Christmas.

While Yvonne finished her bath, Henry got the rest of the presents from her car. Then grabbed his jacket to sit on the deck. While it was cool, the breeze felt nice, and a few minutes of solitude while listening to the tide come in was almost as soothing as knowing Yvonne was his and relaxing in his tub.

"How do you like it?" she said, waking him from a nap he did not know he was taking.

As he turned, he could see she had purchased something for him. A red teddy, with a lace red wrap. He could see the results of the cool air on her skin and replied, "You can buy all the crap you want."

"Sit on the sofa," she said, "I've got a couple more to show you."

Next, she wore a black bra and panty set and this, she asked.

"Much more of this and I'll be joining you in the bedroom," he said as she went back to try on the remaining outfit.

"Don't look till I get in there," she yelled at him.

He didn't look, but he heard the sound of her feet on a hardwood floor. It didn't matter what she had on; it would not make it back to the bedroom. Not on her body anyway.

She had him close his eyes until she was standing in front of him. "Open them," she commanded.

He said nothing.

She was wearing a white bustier which had straps holding up white stockings and a white lace thong.

She reached to grab his hands to help him up, but instead, he pulled her into his lap.

"Do you remember the last time you wore something like this?" he asked.

"Why do you think I put it on last," she whispered in his ear just before her tongue entered.

As he lay her on the sofa, she noticed he had not been sitting on a blanket but on a towel.

"Where did you get this?" she asked, touching the towel.

Before his head disappeared between her thighs, he said in his best imitation of Pam's gravelly voice, "Honey hush, I'm a grown-ass man and I do what I want."

Then his tongue began to tell a story of its own.

"Oh, hell yes you are," she thought.

After he wiped them both off as best he could, they went to shower off. He saw her legs quiver as she stood up, so he carried her to the bathroom. It had taken her ten minutes to get this bustier on; it took him less than a minute to take it off.

Now fully relaxed and in their most comfortable pajamas, they made their way back to the sofa. He stopped by the buffet where his drinks were but picked up a remote control instead.

"What's that for?" she asked.

With the push of a button, the logs in the fireplace were in flame.

"That," he answered.

He sat on the sofa first, leaning against the arm with one leg against the back and the other spread out wide much as hers had been earlier.

"Sit here and lean against me," he said.

As she cuddled up against him with the fire burning and the only other light was the moon's reflection coming through the windows, she thought how lucky she was. That was something she had not considered herself for a long time. Another thought entered her mind as well, no wonder Virginia called him her prince charming.

"We need to go shopping," he said, tearing her away from her romantic thoughts.

"Why?" she spoke.

He thought she sounded a bit annoyed at the question but was unsure what he could have done to provoke that. "I don't have a Christmas tree or any decorations," he said, "next weekend is the first and that's when most people put that sort of thing up, isn't it?"

"Okay," she said, "no more talking, let's just sit here."

It was nice he thought, holding her like this by the light of the moon and the glow of the fire.

He held her in that exact position for an hour and a half until he had to get up to relieve himself.

"Did I fall asleep?" she groggily asked.

"About an hour ago," he replied.

"Why didn't you wake me?"

"You told me to hush."

"Carry me to bed," she asked.

"Your wish is my command," he replied.

She slept naked just as he did, so he removed her clothes and then tucked her in. Once he climbed into bed and the intimate words and kisses were over, she was back asleep before his head was on his pillow.

Chapter 23

For the rest of the time leading up to Christmas, their days were spent with phone calls, dinners, shopping, and lounging around the house. Henry was filled with anticipation; he could not wait until he could give Yvonne her gift. Yvonne was filled with anguish; she didn't have a thing. She could not think of anything and then on the nineteenth, an idea came to her, yes, this is what she would give to him. Her anguish did not go away though because she did not know how he would react. Christmas was still six days away.

This would be the first Christmas Henry would celebrate in this house with Yvonne and all his children. Yvonne had reminded him of his mother when she insisted they all spend it with them. She explained that when the grandkids arrived, she wanted Christmas Day to be celebrated at Grandma's house.

"Henry said he had to run an errand," as Yvonne moved to grab her purse, he said, "not this time."

"Why can't I go?" she asked.

"I told you I would never lie to you so do you want me to answer that question?" he said.

"Yes, I want to know," she said.

"Your Christmas present is ready to be picked up," he answered.

"From where?" she asked. Now she saw the expression his daughter had seen through the years. There was no use in asking any more questions; he was not going to say anything further.

While he was doing that, she remembered she had something she needed to take care of as well.

"How long will you be gone?" she asked.

"About an hour," he replied.

Shortly after Henry left, her mother called. "Are y'all going to be here on Christmas Day?" she asked.

Yvonne didn't think to ask Henry; she just answered they would be there for supper.

"Good," her mother said, "it has been too long since we were together."

Then they began to talk about Henry, their vacation, mostly Yvonne telling her all the ways her life had changed. After a while, Yvonne remembered she had somewhere to go and told her mother she would see her in a couple of days.

When Henry got to the jeweler's he asked how it turned out. Mr. Levy remarked, "I think it looks fantastic but, it is your opinion that counts."

"It is exactly what I wanted it to look like," he said, "but you're wrong about one thing."

"What's that?" Mr. Levy asked.

"I ain't my opinion that counts either, it's hers," Henry replied.

He had another stop to make that he had forgotten about. Days before he had given two photos to a photography studio to see if they could do what he wanted. When they showed him their work it almost brought him to tears.

"This is incredible," he said. "Can you gift wrap them for me?"

In less than fifteen minutes he was on his way. Many years before, Henry and Virginia had stopped buying each other presents instead, focusing their attention on their children. These were the first presents he had bought for his wife in over ten years. These would be the first presents he had ever bought for Yvonne. Now feelings of anxiousness were overcoming him. He liked the presents but would she? This anxiety was even worse than the weeks before when he was waiting for her to be at his door. He knew exactly how that would turn out but now he was second-guessing himself. "Stop!" he yelled at himself in his own head. "She'll like it."

When he got back to his house, Yvonne was not back; Elaine and Ryan were. "To what do I owe the pleasure of your company?" he asked jokingly.

"Where is Yvonne?" Elaine asked.

He grabbed his phone, "where are you?" he asked.

"Ok see you soon, love you."

"She is turning on Butler Avenue, be here in a couple of minutes."

"Then we'll wait," Elaine said.

Yvonne saw Elaine and Ryan standing in the living room with her father on the sofa.

"Come join Dad on the sofa," Elaine said.

When Yvonne was seated, Elaine blurted out, "we're pregnant."

"Y'all finally quit practicing so much," was how Henry responded.

Yvonne stood up and hugged Elaine in the way Virginia would have hugged her. This stepmom/grandma stuff was going to be fun, she thought.

Elaine and Ryan left to go tell his parents. This would be their first grandchild too.

When his children left, Yvonne asked where her gift was.

"Is it Christmas Day?" he replied.

"I don't see any new presents under the tree," she said.

Now he laughed, "well I got it and you ain't touching it till I give it to you."

"I'll show you mine if you show me yours," she smiled while asking.

"That is exactly how it worked last time except you snuck up on me to see mine," he said.

She had been talking about presents; he meant something else entirely. But it was true, she thought.

Thursday, they went to eat at the VFW. Nate had always said it was a bunch of old guys reliving their glory days but, while there were older guys there, there were as many men from the wars in Iraq and Afghanistan as there were from Vietnam. Much to her surprise, the evening was very enjoyable. Colonel Patrick seemed to be particularly happy to meet her. He told her about the day Virginia died and remembered thinking he would be attending another funeral soon.

"You saved him," the Colonel said.

"We saved each other," she replied.

Every person there understood the pin she wore. Most people had no idea it meant the loss of a child or spouse but everyone at the VFW did.

Yvonne told Henry the third Thursday of the month had a permanent appointment.

"For what?" he asked, looking completely ignorant.

"Here silly, at the VFW," she answered while smacking his arm.

Friday, it rained; each minute of Friday felt like forever.

On Saturday, Elaine and Ryan invited them to dinner.

Sunday, they went to church with her parents. A couple of the people who knew the Brown family were distant to Henry, and one of Yvonne's cousins was rude, plainly asking Henry if Yvonne was too young for him.

Henry sternly replied, "what business is that of yours?"

Monday at least would see the arrival of Bubba and Loni. Yvonne offered them the condo so they wouldn't have to drive five hours on Christmas Day.

They had discussed what to do with the condo; Henry was

completely helpless, saying it was hers to decide. Neither selling nor renting it appealed to her very much. She was hoping an answer would wash up on the beach much like Henry had.

That evening was so nice, the four of them enjoying dinner, discussing the arrival of someone that they all now knew would be named Virginia. Yvonne was planning baby showers with Loni, while William and his father were watching football. Once the game was over, not by time but based on the score, William and Loni left to enjoy the balcony of Yvonne's condo.

Yvonne then asked Henry if they could open their presents now.

He laughed, saying she was like a child at Christmas.

She explained she had not felt like this since she was about ten.

"Why ten?" he asked.

"My father had told me when I was eight that I could not have a go-cart until I was ten."

"Isn't that an unusual present for a girl?" he asked.

"My father never treated me like a girl," she said sadly, "until my tits grew."

Henry laughed at that, "those are hard to look past," he said, "what happened after that?"

"He began to ignore me," she replied.

"I'm sorry, little girls can be difficult for men to deal with, particularly if they wanted a son."

"I don't think that's it," she replied, "it was because I started to look like my mother. She had to have an emergency C-Section with me and then a hysterectomy to stop her bleeding."

"Damn, that's awful," he said.

"Anyway, I was ten, the year I got my go-cart. In fact, it is still in the garage at my parent's house."

"So, can we, please open just one?"

There was no way he could say no to her now.

"If the tears started, he would let her open them all."

She did not know about his kryptonite yet, and he did not want her to find out any sooner than she would, "damn," he thought, "I bet Elaine already told her."

Elaine had in fact told Yvonne her father was a big soft teddy bear. "If you argue with him, he likes that, and you will always lose. If you drop one tear, he is done." They both laughed as she said it.

Her emotions now were her own with no purpose of manipulation. "Please," she asked.

Henry started towards the Christmas tree, "what are you doing?" she asked.

He stopped and said, "okay then how are we opening presents if I can't get yours?"

Yvonne had also hidden a present in the tree; she thought he had seen it and that was why she had stopped him. When he reached for a small box in the back of the tree, she realized he had not seen her or at least pretended not to see hers.

When she opened the box, tears flowed like Niagara Falls. "Oh my God, it is beautiful," she said. "Did you have this made for me?" It was a choker-type necklace that was just long enough to allow the charm to sit at the base of her throat. The charm was a compass rose set in gold, and all the points and rays were made of Emeralds. Instead of it being oriented with the attachment at the North position, it was at the East position. The direction they had been looking the day they met and got married. Henry put it on her so she could see it in the mirror. Perhaps she didn't like it, but he sometimes would regret buying it. Several times he bit the necklace instead of her neck because she would never take it off.

"Ok," Yvonne said, now she walked back to the tree and reached around but at a much lower level. "This is for you, guess what it is?"

"I hate this game," he said, "Virginia would always have me guess, and the disappointment on her face when I was correct ruined the entire experience for me."

"I'm not Virginia," she said, "guess."

The box was the size and shape he recognized. He remembered what he had told her about his watch, so it looked like she had replaced it. "A watch," he said.

Yvonne tried to look disappointed but could not. "Open it," she demanded.

It was not a watch.

His mind was running through everything he knew when it suddenly hit him like a ton of bricks.

This was an Early Pregnancy Test, and the window revealed a pink plus sign. He was still staring at it when she said that was where she went the day he went to get her gift, to confirm it with the doctor.

There was only a blank expression. His eyes were fixed on the gift.

She said, "say something," as a tear fell from her eye.

"Oh my God," he yelled as he grabbed Yvonne, spinning her around the room. "I am so in love with you right now, who else knows?"

"No one," she said.

"Oh my God," he said again as the reality of this new set in. "I am going to have a child younger than my grandkids."

"And I am going to be a mother," she said, now tears were freely flowing.

"I thought only rock stars had children in their fifties," he said.

She smiled, touching her charm, "bet they can't make a woman orgasm like you can."

"That sounds like an invitation," he said, carrying her to the bedroom.

Chapter 24

The next day brought more joy than any of them had ever experienced. The house was filled with laughter that could not be diminished. The gifts were opened, but the news of the new arrivals, particularly for Yvonne, simply increased the happiness each family had for each other.

The next days turned into weeks, then months. There were doctor visits, showers, and parties, and with each passing day, the anticipation grew.

On April seventeenth, Virginia Ann made her arrival. St. Mary's Hospital in Athens had been the birthplace of her father, and amazingly the same doctor delivered her. On his wall were several photos of new babies held by the parents he had delivered as well. In two and a half years, he would also get to deliver William the third.

June thirtieth brought the arrival of Annabel Elizabeth. Similarly, Memorial Hospital was only forty miles from Ft. Stewart and Winn Army Hospital where Elaine had been born.

It was only sixteen days till Yvonne's due date. The summer heat, as well as her excitement over becoming a grandmother, only heightened her anticipation of her upcoming delivery. Also, it was the week of the Fourth of July, with Saturday being the end of Henry's vow to Virginia.

They had decided to spend the night of July third at her condo so her trip out on the sand with him would not be so difficult. Although she had only gained twenty pounds through her pregnancy, her joints were beginning to loosen in preparation for childbirth.

The morning of the fourth was a beautiful sunrise, much like most mornings. As the sun began to rise, they stood there, arm in arm, both understanding that a year ago this day only brought despair. Today, there was a happiness and contentment they could not measure. When the sun cleared the horizon, Yvonne spoke.

"Virginia was right, this is the most beautiful spot on the face of the earth, and I think I need to get to the hospital."

"It is still almost two weeks till your due date," Henry said.

"I don't think Carlton is waiting till then," she said wincing.

At two thirty in the afternoon, on the Fourth of July, Carlton Blake made his arrival. There had been no complications or prolonged labor. Yvonne had been able to deliver him with an epidural so when he arrived the nurse placed him directly on her breast. Women did this every day she thought but, "I have given birth to the most beautiful boy in the world."

"If I died today," Yvonne stated, "my life would be complete."

"Well, you'd better get well fast," Henry smiled, "I hate changing diapers." Between Yvonne, Bibi, Elaine, and Loni, he would not have to worry about that.

The nurses in the delivery room had been giggling through the entire birth, to what was a mystery until Yvonne asked Henry exactly how long he was going to wear that outfit?

He had not changed clothes or considered what he was wearing.

"Damn," he thought, "I look like an idiot."

One of the nurses laughingly asked him what occasion was being celebrated.

When he explained that today marked a year since he refused to wear the outfit for his wife, her death the next day, as well as his vow. Any thoughts of laughter were removed from all who were present.

Henry then left to go out to the waiting room as Carlton was being taken to the nursery for viewing. Waiting for a glimpse of their first grandchild were Harold and Bibi, beside them was Karen.

"How is Yvonne," Bibi implored.

"Everyone is doing great," Henry answered, "and they will be opening the curtain any minute now." Henry could see the expression on Harry's face was much as he must have looked months prior. Becoming a grandfather was incredibly different than becoming a father. He knew that better than anyone, he had become a grandfather only four days ago and now a father again. It was different though; he had been in his twenties when he first became a father knowing nothing of the challenges that would involve. Also, there had been his and Virginia's parents to help. That duty would belong to Harold and Bibi alone. He was thinking what his father would have said when the curtain came open revealing

Carlton to his new grandparents. His father's voice echoed in his head, "Son, do you know what causes this?"

Henry went back in to sit with Yvonne until she could be taken to a private room for the family to gather and hold the new arrival.

Everyone was waiting when the nurse wheeled Carlton into the room. To everyone's surprise, no one could prevent Harry from holding his grandson first. Realizing this child was as safe as any child on earth could be, the nurse excused herself, leaving them to take turns holding the baby. After only seconds, Bibi took Carlton and walked him over to the bed sitting beside Yvonne.

"Now you know how I felt," Bibi said, "there is no better feeling in the world."

Yvonne smiled through her and Bibi's tears; she had a feeling of contentment that can only be felt by a mother after giving birth to her first child. Whether or not she ever had more children, there was no way this feeling could ever be duplicated. As Yvonne was thinking there can only be one first kiss, one first date, one first..., she looked up and saw Henry's face. He had not been her first anything. Yet the love and fulfillment he had brought to her life matched anything she and Nate had shared. He was in fact her second husband but, was also the father of her first child. Being second in the husband category was the only category he was second in, and if this was true with husbands, it could be true with a second child. She would never have an answer to that question though Carlton would be her only child.

Throughout everything, Karen was silent. As thrilling as this day was for everyone else, it only served as a reminder that she was alone. Yvonne had two men who had loved her passionately and was now a mother, these things had never happened for her, and she thought it never would. It was difficult for her to smile. When finally, Yvonne offered Carlton to Karen, he opened his eyes and to Karen at least, looked like he smiled.

It was a look that she had never seen from a man. This was complete, total, pure, unequivocal love with no conditions. She might never have a husband, but she could become a mother, was what she thought. Karen was looking at Henry while holding his son. His expression was different than when he had looked at anyone else holding Carlton, he could not help but notice how much Karen looked like Virginia and seeing her holding his son brought back memories of Virginia holding William.

"Birkenstocks," she thought. Henry was a pair of Birkenstocks. He was the kind of man that did not need accessories. She had owned several pairs of Birkenstocks before but only bought new ones when the old ones fell apart. It was the only shoe, she thought, that had no purpose except to make the wearer feel good. "Yes," Henry was a pair of Birkenstocks, a type of man she had never dated but, definitely father material. Karen took Carlton back to Yvonne and as she handed him over whispered to her that when she got home there was something she wanted to speak to her about.

"What is it?" Yvonne said quietly.

"Never mind right now, you just get well," Karen smiled as she said.

It struck Yvonne this was the first time she had seen Karen smile.

Yvonne was released after forty-eight hours, so Henry prepared to take them back to their home. "Damn," he thought, "I'm going to have to sell my little sporty car." He knew Yvonne would never let him sell the truck, but it had a bench seat and while it could hold a car seat, it wasn't very practical. Yvonne's car was too small; besides, it drove like the engine was about to give out. It did have four doors, so they would use her car until they decided what to buy. Yvonne told him to give her time to think about it. She rarely made snap decisions or regretted them.

After the baby was fastened, Yvonne in her seat, Henry went to get in the car. The nurse who helped them looked at him as if he were stealing something.

"She just had a baby, no hanky-panky for eight weeks," she said sternly.

All he could think to say was, "Yes, Ma'am."

He immediately remembered telling Yvonne she would have to tone down the noise she made during their love-making sessions or risk waking the grandchildren. Now there would be a child in the house all the time he thought. He was thinking how unfair it was that his love life would be taking such a drastic turn for the worse even though they were still newlyweds. Apparently, his expression conveyed every thought directly to Yvonne.

"Don't worry," she said with a big smile, "I don't think we will have any trouble finding a babysitter, and eight weeks will fly."

Bibi never said no to babysitting Carlton, and the time did fly, but Yvonne was more than ready for the gift Henry had for her birthday; four weeks was long enough, they thought.

The nineteenth was VFW night. Henry said he would stay home, but Yvonne insisted he go to share pictures of his new son with everyone. Besides, Karen would be coming by, so they would be fine. Henry left at six thirty, and Karen arrived at seven thirty. It didn't take long before Karen reminded Yvonne about the day Carlton was born; she had something to discuss.

"Yvonne," said Karen, "okay, tell me the news."

"Well, it really is not news, it is a request like I have never asked of anyone before," Karen replied. Yvonne could see the serious expression on Karen's face, realizing whatever it was must be important.

"When I came to the hospital to see you become a mother something happened to me," Karen started to explain. "Never have I had regrets about not being married, especially witnessing everything you went through before you met Henry. But, when I saw you lying on that bed and particularly when I held your son, for the first time in my life, I felt truly alone."

"So, what are you telling me?" Yvonne asked.

"I want to have a baby," Karen replied.

Everything Karen had just told her began to turn into a question she was hoping, she was praying, Karen would not ask.

"With whom?" Yvonne said.

"I would like Henry to be my sperm donor," Karen said.

Yvonne was almost yelling, "Have you asked him?"

"No, I would never do that, I am here asking you first," Karen replied with a pained expression.

"Why him?" Yvonne was on the verge of becoming furious.

"Because I have never met anyone like him," Karen said. "I will never have a man look at me the way Henry looks at you." Then Karen continued, "You have been married to two incredible men, while I have never met a man who was interested in anything more than getting me naked. I know that there are plenty of sperm donors, but they would all be men just like the ones who have already entered my life and left. I want my baby to be like yours, I have always wanted to be like you. Yvonne, you have everything, and I have nothing. I don't want to grow old alone."

They both sat in silence. Yvonne had never seen Karen like this. She was almost hysterical.

"Please just consider it," Karen continued, "I promise there will never come a time when you or Henry would ever be intruded on by me, and I will never speak to who the child's father is or ask for anything."

Yvonne was still staring at Karen, completely speechless, unbelieving she would have the nerve to ask for such a thing.

She was about to tell Karen to get out when the elevator door opened.

The tension in the room was incredible when Henry exclaimed, "How are you ladies doing?"

The abruptness with which Yvonne said, "Karen has something to ask you, let him know what the answer was before the question was finished."

While Henry was still trying to process the reason for the tone in Yvonne's voice.

Karen blurted out, "I want to have a baby and for you to be the sperm donor."

Henry knew his answer should have been an immediate no, but the shock of these two women that had been friends for decades caused him to look at them both in complete disbelief due to the request that had just been made. While it was only seconds, it was seconds too long for Yvonne.

"Are you thinking about it?" Yvonne yelled at him.

"I am having trouble thinking about anything right now," he said, "you've never yelled at me like that before."

Karen was now getting up to leave and she said, "I didn't want to cause a fight between the two of you, I just don't want to grow old alone."

"Well," Yvonne said, "no matter what Henry thinks or says the answer is NO!"

When Karen had left, Henry went to sit beside Yvonne who told him to sit across from her.

"What did I do?" Henry asked.

"You didn't say no fast enough," she said with a forced smile.

Henry got down on his knees, crawling to where she was sitting.

"You have to admit that in a million years was not a question I was expecting to hear," he said apologetically.

Then he began to say words that he would teach Carlton to say to calm her mood.

"You're sweet."

"You're beautiful."

"I love you." Placing a kiss on her cheek.

Then he put his arms around her neck before finishing, "you're the best wife/mommy in the world."

His words worked now as they would always work with their son. She knew her reaction was harsh, but Henry was hers and not anyone else's.

Carlton began to cry; it was time for his supper.

Henry was amazed that his wife's large breasts were now even larger. He was also jealous of having to share them with his boy. That wouldn't last forever though he knew then these newer larger breasts would return to their rightful owner. Henry just sat there watching her nurse their son. He was sure there was not a more beautiful woman on the planet.

"I love you, gorgeous," he said.

"And I love you," Yvonne replied, smiling now that her anger was subsiding.

After their goodnight kisses, each also kissing the new baby who would sleep in a crib beside their bed, Yvonne drifted off to sleep thinking her life was perfectly complete. There could never be anything to make her happier than she was right now.

Henry fell asleep hoping their lives would not meet dire tragedies as their former lives had. He would not make the same mistakes he made with his first two children, and he would love this woman as best he could for the rest of their lives...

There was nothing for Jimmy to write next. The story Henry and Yvonne finished telling him ended with their lives close to the present day. The problem was he was certain that this was not an ending, at least not one he wanted to write. Many years ago, partly out of necessity and partly out of intention, he had learned to be patient. This was a story that was not over. Time needed to pass and events that were yet to unfold needed to happen. He was certain of a couple of things. Henry was an incredibly determined man and if it were in his power, this story would take years to unfold. Carlton was a little boy and if possible, his parents would make sure his life was filled with love. The other certainty was no one in this story was going anywhere. They were all tied to this place like he had become. In time he was sure that the story would find its way to a resolution. Until then he would take a printed copy of the manuscript and place it in his desk. Normally, his writing was kept on his computer but, in this case, he wanted a backup just in case.

What he could not know was that it would indeed be years before he knew how the story would end. After he placed the copy in his desk drawer, he was not sure where his writing would take him next. Jimmy was comfortable with the limitations of his creativity, a tangent to a story he knew was not difficult but, producing a story entirely out of whole cloth was something entirely different.

He decided that he would not look for something to write, he would leave it up to others. Every day he spent time in the cemetery and often walked around Savannah in the parks and squares.

He had not sought out Wes, he was simply running in the cemetery. Wes had invited him to sit and listen to his story. There were now three novels, Good Fortune and Spider Lily which had been published, and a movie about his first novel because he chose to listen to the story. Compelling stories were everywhere, he just needed to look for the same expression on a person's face that he had seen in Wes, then persuade them that he was someone they could share their story with who was trustworthy.

He thought his life was full. There was a level of happiness and contentment that he had never known. The satisfaction he knew from his work, his family, and the place he now lived was expressed to the world. He could not see the person he was becoming, always he worried about the man he had formerly been and was determined to never let those doubts and fears control him again. Perhaps it was this self-fulfillment, or the joy from his wife and children, or his newly gained confidence but, whether single or combined, the world did not see him the way he saw himself.

In a couple of months, there would be a woman named Stacey sitting on a bench in Pulaski Square downtown. To Jimmy, she had the expression of a woman who was lost and foundering. To her, Jimmy looked like the adult version of a boy she had known as a teen, strong, confident, and filled with compassion. What neither of them knew was their lives would never be the same.

It would be a while before he wrote another novel. What he could not know was he was about to find other people with Love Lessons and his next work would be a collection of short stories.

www.ingramcontent.com/pod-product-compliance
Lightning Source LLC
Chambersburg PA
CBHW071506140726
47997CB00005B/1875